Praise for Dana Marie Bell's
Dare to Believe

"I wholeheartedly recommend Dare to Believe to anyone who wants to take a short vacation from reality."

~ *Whipped Cream Reviews*

"Everything about this story is fantastic. All of the characters are interesting, even those that are extremely unlikable, and their presence enriches the story. The ending is immensely satisfying and leaves this reader anxiously awaiting the next book in the series."

~ *The Romance Studio*

"...an intense and intriguing story... I'm looking forward to the other books in the series, one featuring Shane and also their sister, Moira."

~ *The Good, The Bad and The Unread*

"With a series of hotter than hot men crossing the pages and spunky, tell-it-like-it is women standing up to them you'll love every sentence."

~ *Manic Readers*

Look for these titles by
Dana Marie Bell

Now Available:

Halle Pumas Series
The Wallflower
Sweet Dreams
Cat of a Different Color
Steel Beauty
Only in My Dreams

True Destiny Series
Very Much Alive

The Gray Court Series
Dare To Believe (Book 1)

Print Anthology
Hunting Love

Dare to Believe

Dana Marie Bell

A Samhain Publishing, Ltd. publication.

Samhain Publishing, Ltd.
577 Mulberry Street, Suite 1520
Macon, GA 31201
www.samhainpublishing.com

Dare to Believe
Copyright © 2010 by Dana Marie Bell
Print ISBN: 978-1-60504-729-4
Digital ISBN: 978-1-60504-632-7

Cover by Tuesday Dube

This book is a work of fiction. The names, characters, places, and incidents are products of the writer's imagination or have been used fictitiously and are not to be construed as real. Any resemblance to persons, living or dead, actual events, locale or organizations is entirely coincidental.

All Rights Are Reserved. No part of this book may be used or reproduced in any manner whatsoever without written permission, except in the case of brief quotations embodied in critical articles and reviews.

First Samhain Publishing, Ltd. electronic publication: July 2009
First Samhain Publishing, Ltd. print publication: May 2010

Dedication

To Mom, guess what? He lied to you. I don't care what he says, Dad DOES have scooter envy.

To Dad, just admit it. It will be better in the long run. You're jealous because I have a headlamp and I beat you in that race. Come to the dark side. Resistance is futile. Besides, we have cookies.

To Dusty, thank you for daring to believe in me.

And to the woman who wrote our beautiful wedding vows over ten years ago. I hope you won't mind that I adjusted them to be the binding of a Sidhe lord and his mate. Even today I read those words and smile. To me, they really were magical.

Chapter One

"You want me to wear *that*?"

"Shhh. Honey, this would look gorgeous on you."

Ruby stared at the skimpy outfit Mandy waved in front of her like a red cape. The move was totally appropriate since Ruby would feel like a cow in it. "Don't they have a lovely pumpkin costume? Oh! How about a pony? I could probably pull off a pony."

Mandy glared at her. "You have a body most women would die for. You're curvy, not fat."

"No. Seriously. How about one of those robe thingies? With a hood! I could get a rubber knife and be an evil sorceress slash human sacrificer!"

"Ruby! Knock it off." Mandy tapped one foot impatiently at Ruby's attempts to get around her. "Try it on. I guarantee you'll look incredible."

"I'm short and fat, Mandy. *Short* and *fat*. There is no way I can get away with that costume and not look like a complete idiot."

Ruby made one last attempt to move towards the evil sorceress robes, only to have Mandy hold up the red devil costume with an evil grin. The red leather miniskirt, red satin corset and red horns looked like something the blonde, beautiful Mandy could get away with. Short, well-endowed Ruby would look like a moron.

"C'mon, Ruby." Mandy rocked the outfit, grinning wickedly. "I dare you."

Oh, no. "No, Mandy." Ruby turned away from the costume, praying she got away fast enough before her oldest friend said—

"Double-dog dare you."

Aw hell.

She never could turn down a double-dog dare. Mandy had gotten her into more trouble with those three little words than anyone knew. Mandy was the one who'd double-dog dared Ruby to go out with Bobby in the eleventh grade, though she'd long since apologized. She'd dared Ruby to get even when Bobby had bragged all over school that he'd "scored, but she was a lousy fuck". That double-dog dare led to The Pencil Dick Poster Incident that had gotten Ruby two weeks' suspension and a stag trip to the prom. In college, she'd found herself walking backwards for an entire day, just to prove she could. That had earned her a free meal at her favorite restaurant, though, so that one had been worth it.

Childish? Yeah. But she just couldn't resist when a dare was thrown out, especially the way Mandy did it. *I can almost hear the chickens clucking in the background.*

Ruby huffed out a breath and turned. Mandy had added thigh-high black leather boots and a black leather belt. A red velvet choker with a dangling black glass gem completed the look. She grinned and waved the outfit in Ruby's face.

"Oh, great. I'll be a demonic hooker." Ruby raised one cynical brow and put her hands on her hips. "I suppose you'll be going as an angel?"

Mandy's eyes went wide. "Oh, I like that idea. Wait right here." And Mandy took off, dropping the Sexy Little Devil outfit

Dare to Believe

to the floor. Ruby picked up the bustier and held it to her ample breasts with a sigh. *It's going to be a long party.* Watching Leo with whatever blonde he'd decided to bring would just be the topper on what she just knew was going to be a pretty crappy evening.

She had to stop wondering what Leo would think of the outfit. There was no sense in it. Leo Dunne, CEO of Fantasy Events, had women literally throwing themselves at him. The man had everything going for him. Black hair, brilliant green eyes and a body to die for all wrapped up in Armani, he epitomized tall, dark and handsome. Why the hell would a man like that look twice at five-foot-nothing Ruby?

True, she wasn't exactly a beer goggle, but she wasn't the tall, thin, blonde model type Leo was known to escort around town. It was just too bad she had a huge crush on him. She needed to get over it and move on. Maybe she'd say yes to the date Mark in accounting kept asking her for. He might not be Leo, but he *was* cute, and, more importantly, available.

Out of the corner of her eye she saw a tall, dark-haired man exiting the costume shop, and her heart nearly stopped. *Leo? Nah. Couldn't be.* Every tall, dark-haired man looked like Leo these days.

She snorted in disgust. Mandy had managed to find the exact same outfit in white and silver, complete with tinsel halo. Looked like she was stuck going to the party in the demon girl outfit. She picked up the rest of the costume off the floor and followed Mandy to the registers.

Maybe I don't need a date. Maybe I need therapy. A twelve-step program to get over my addiction to Leo Dunne. She purchased the devil outfit with a grimace, ignoring Mandy's satisfied smirk. She grabbed the bag from the gum-snapping teenager, smiling weakly in response to the clerk's "Happy

Halloween!" Mandy made her purchase and the two women made their way out of the store. "I'm starved." Mandy looked up and down the street before crossing. "How about we go for margaritas and Mexican? We can call some of the girls and have a night out."

Oh, yeah. Now that's my kind of therapy. "Sounds great. Let's go." She got into Mandy's white convertible with a happy bounce, eager for good food, a drink or two, and the comfort of her friends. With any luck Leo would stay out of her thoughts.

Her head thudded onto the backrest. *And maybe ducks will fly out of my butt.*

Leo looked around at the Halloween party and nodded. This one was strictly for employees of Fantasy Events, a thank you for all of the hard work they'd put in that year, and so far everyone seemed to be having a good time. Almost all of his employees and their significant others had shown up. They were even in costume. Fantasy Events didn't do an office Christmas party. They usually didn't have the time, with all of the parties Fantasy Events coordinated around that holiday. So this was their yearly bash, and he made the most of it.

It was his favorite time of year, filled with everyone's fantasies. And as an added bonus it was the one day a year when he could go to the office without a shirt on and not get arrested for indecent exposure or sued for sexual harassment.

No children had been invited. This was an adult-only party, and it showed. A few people had definitely had too much to drink already, so he was glad he'd contracted rooms in the hotel for anyone who felt they couldn't drive home that night. Music played loudly, making conversation almost impossible. Couples danced together on the floor, laughing and talking. Little groups

Dare to Believe

dotted the area around the dancers, enjoying the buffet dinner he'd had catered.

It was going well, other than one little thing. *She* wasn't there yet. Ruby Halloway, the woman who'd haunted his dreams for months. He turned, wondering where his personal siren was. The party had started over an hour ago, and Ruby and Mandy were nowhere in sight. He wondered if she'd decided to bail on Mandy. He hoped not. He was dying to see her in that red corset. He stifled a smile, remembering how she'd held it up to her chest, looking so uncertain. It had taken all of his willpower to stop himself from going to her then and there. He'd longed to soothe her but was afraid she'd once again disappear just like she always did.

It had taken years to find her. When he'd first come into the company, he'd caught the faint, elusive scent that so drew him now. Maybe if he hadn't been so busy learning the business and meeting with clients he might have put more effort into pursuing that scent and finding the woman who now held all of his attention, waking and dreaming. Instead he'd wasted all of that time. Oh, he'd hardly been celibate in the last five years. He'd dated plenty of women. Just none of them had been *her*. The one woman created by the universe just for him.

It wasn't until he'd already become CEO, taking over for the previous owner of the Washington, DC events' company, that he'd finally caught a glimpse of her. Ruby Halloway. He'd been walking down the hallway in Accounting, talking to her boss, when Leo stopped dead. She'd been bent over a drawer, pulling out a file. The tight denim had stretched across the most luscious ass it had ever been his pleasure to see. He'd longed to walk over, cup that ass, and claim the owner before she knew what hit her.

And then he'd caught her scent. He'd almost moaned at the savage rush of erotic heat. It was only his employee's nudges that had made him realize where he was. He'd immediately asked who the woman was.

She'd heard her name, started, and taken off for parts unknown before he could get an introduction. She'd been doing it ever since. As soon as she knew he was there, she either hid or left. It was driving him insane. He'd managed to hide his presence from her once or twice, and caught glimpses of the warm, funny woman she truly was. He'd finally called in the cavalry in the form of Mandy, who'd been delighted to set up her shy best friend.

He'd have made his move sooner if it hadn't been for Kaitlynn Malmayne and the negotiations with the Malmayne family. Hopefully she now understood that Leo was unavailable for anything she might want from him. He'd finally gotten Kaitlynn and her posse back on the plane to L.A. It was time, past time, to claim his woman.

Tonight he was going to do everything in his power to see to it that this time Ruby had no reason to run. He turned in place again, sighing in disappointment.

If I can find her, that is.

When he finally saw her, he nearly choked. The two women stood together, looking around. They'd obviously just arrived, and were checking the party out, seeing who was there. Mandy wore a white leather miniskirt, white satin corset, silver belt, and white choker with a silver charm dangling from it. Her thigh-high white leather boots had four-inch heels, making her already impressive height even more impressive. White strips of cloth dangled from two wires protruding from her back, and Leo figured they were meant to represent wings. A silver halo gleamed above the golden curls that drifted across her shoulders.

Peeking out from behind her white wings was the sexiest

little devil Leo had ever seen.

She wore the same exact outfit Mandy did, but in red and black. Gleaming red satin cupped the smooth golden globes of her breasts. Red leather clung to her hips. Black thigh-high boots hugged those delicious legs. Tiny red horns peeked out from her reddish brown hair. A black bit of glass dangled from the red choker surrounding her slender throat. She looked terrified. He studied her face, feeling a sense of completion that never failed to stun him.

She was the most beautiful woman in the room.

Dark brown brows arched delicately over a pair of sherry eyes tipped with the darkest, longest lashes he'd ever seen. Her nose had a slight tilt at the end. She nibbled anxiously at her full bottom lip, her high cheekbones flushed with excitement and trepidation. Her eyes darted around the room, searching for something or someone.

Mandy pulled Ruby out from behind her and shoved her into the room with a grip that would do a cop proud. Ruby glared at her friend and wiggled, obviously trying to pull her arm free. That little jiggle did things for her body that had to be illegal in several states.

He suddenly wished his leather pants weren't quite so tight. His body saluted the little devil, straining against the leather. When she took a deep breath, those amazing breasts pushed up and out of the corset, forcing Leo to swallow a groan.

Damn. Talking Mandy into giving him a hand getting Ruby to relax had been seriously worth it. The woman who'd haunted his dreams for months looked incredible. Even under the shapeless clothes she wore to the office he'd known she was sweetly rounded, just the way he liked his women. Ruby had generous breasts that begged for a man's hands and mouth, hips you could hold on to while riding her to oblivion, and an ass he'd die to sink his teeth into. Voluptuous, that was the word. And her scent. That vanilla and peaches scent that drifted around her wherever she went. It was enough to drive him insane. Hell, he'd passed a bakery on his way home the other night and gotten hard just smelling the vanilla scents drifting out the door. Damn the Malmaynes! If it wasn't for them he would have been after her a hell of a lot sooner. Escorting Kaitlynn around town and showing her the sights had bored the spit out of him. Kaitlynn's saccharine sweetness was like nails on a chalkboard, not that he'd tell the blonde princess that. And her sycophantic, selfish cousins were even worse.

If he had to even look at another leggy, flat-chested, half-starved, self-absorbed socialite he'd go stark raving mad.

Now he just had to convince his shy little devil to take a chance on him. He moved through the crowd, determined to claim her before anyone else could.

Ruby glared at Mandy, wondering if a jury would convict her if she killed her best friend. Mandy merely grinned and nudged her again, causing Ruby to lose her balance in those damned four-inch heels.

"Oh!" She squealed, preparing herself for a fall to the hard wooden floor.

Instead, she landed on a hard, bare chest. An incredibly hot bare chest. The best male chest she'd ever felt before in her life. She had to resist the urge to pet and stroke the rock hard muscles rippling under that silky skin.

"Sorry," she muttered, feeling herself turn red. She risked a peek up.

And up. The owner of the chest was tall. Her head barely topped his shoulders in her four inch heels. She nibbled again at her bottom lip, her eyes tracing their way up to the face above the chest.

Oh boy.

Leo Dunne's green eyes twinkled down at her, his arms like steel bands around her waist. "Hello, Ruby." The satisfaction in his voice was strange. The deep, possessive rumble sent a shiver down her spine.

Her cheeks heated up when she realized just how close she was plastered to his body. She pushed against that smooth, hot flesh. He released her with flattering reluctance, his hands lingering on her hips even when she pushed back to a standing position.

"Um, hi." Ruby mentally winced at the lame reply and stared up into the amused, heated eyes of the CEO.

Heated?

"Would you like to dance?" His hands flexed on her hips, holding her even more tightly. She got the distinct impression the question wasn't really a question.

"You almost have to," Mandy's amused voice came from her elbow. "The two of you match."

Ruby blinked and took a closer look at Leo's costume. He wore tight black leather pants, black leather boots with lots of shiny silver buckles, and not much else. A pair of red and black devil horns peeked out from his dark hair. In one ear a ruby stud gleamed.

Ruby shot one quick glare at Mandy. Somehow she wasn't buying her best friend's innocent act. Add in that Mandy knew all about her crush on Leo, *and* that she was close friends with the man's secretary, and she had to wonder if Mandy had somehow set her up to match the hunky CEO. "You know, I'm not sure I *can* dance in these boots," Ruby muttered. She wondered how quickly she could get away from Satan before she made a complete fool of herself and drooled all over him.

She also wondered where his date was. If she was really lucky she'd be able to duck away before whatever blonde he was with saw them and ripped her hair out by the roots.

"Double-dog dare ya." Mandy chuckled wickedly.

Aw hell. Here we go again.

Ruby's spine straightened, her eyes snapping with annoyance and determination. She seized his hand and practically dragged him onto the dance floor. She might not be able to dance in those heels but she could sure as hell stomp in them.

He was grateful to his guardian angel back there, but what the hell was *that* all about?

She turned in his arms in the middle of the dance floor and slapped her hands onto his shoulders hard enough to make him wince. He tried to get her to move with him, but her body didn't bend. It was like dancing with an exotic piece of wood. Gorgeous but stiff.

"Relax, Ruby. I don't bite." *Much*, he thought.

She glared up at him. "Does your date?"

He smiled, slow and hungry. "I came alone."

"Oh."

If anything, his answer made her tense up more. The only good part of the dance was the way her satin-covered breasts kept brushing against his chest. He saw the way her nipples beaded and his erection grew even more painful behind the tight leather pants. Thanks to the fact that he was at least a foot taller than Ruby he could see all that wonderful cleavage the corset displayed to maximum advantage. He had a hard time keeping his eyes on her face; hell, a saint would have peeked. She tried to control her breathing, but he could tell she was just as aroused as he was.

And she was trying desperately to hide it.

The music shifted into something low and sultry, tempting him into holding her even closer. He leaned down towards her and whispered in her ear on impulse, his voice deliberately low. "Relax and dance with me. I double-dog dare you."

She jumped. *"Relax and dance with me. I double-dog dare you."*

Shit.

She stared up at him and saw the sexy male satisfaction teasing the corners of his lips. His expression was still heated, drifting lazily from her face to her breasts, the dare he'd just issued vivid in his gaze. He didn't think she'd go through with it, and it showed. Warm curls of excitement unfurled deep in the pit of her stomach. Desire, so rarely aimed at her, held her in its arms. She felt an answering flame deep in the center of her being, challenging her to accept what he was so obviously offering.

For once, just this once, she was going to go with it, and to hell with the voices in her head telling her he was only playing with someone like her.

She allowed the desire she felt to unfurl deep within her. She felt it stretch itself, curling through her being like a sensuous cat, causing her nipples to tighten in anticipation. Her panties dampened in response to the heat in his eyes. Her muscles relaxed, caught up in the tingles moving through her whole body. She let her eyelids droop and looked up at him from beneath her lashes. "Like this?"

Was that sultry whisper my voice? The sane accountant part of her brain was shocked. The wicked little devil that danced in Leo's arms chortled gleefully as she let her inner sex kitten out to play.

She began to move to the music. Her hips began to sway, causing her stomach to caress his erection. *Oh wow. Is that for me?* The feel of his desire only heightened her own. Her breasts rubbed against his chest in a sultry invitation. Her arms reached up languidly to encircle his neck, her fingers tangling in his dark hair, she moved. She closed her eyes, the better to enjoy the music, her face tilted up to his in unconscious invitation. She licked her lips, leaving them wet and pouting and ripe.

"*Damn.*" The curse was a husky groan, and her lips curved. One of his hands began stroking up and down her back, moving her body in time to his. She opened her eyes when his hand caressed her ass. His head was tilted down over hers possessively. His other hand kept her firmly up against him, his fingers splayed in her hair. His normal suave mask was gone, leaving behind the look of a hungry predator.

Holy shit. Her entire body was on fire. He moved one of her hands down to his chest, cradling it in his own. She couldn't help but caress him, opening her hand to feel the muscles undulating against her palm. Those hard planes and wicked muscles were covered in the finest, warmest silk she'd ever been privileged to touch. His hair was soft, cool to the touch, an erotic counterpoint to the strength in his back and neck. When she felt him bend down to her it didn't even occur to her to pull back. The thought of finally tasting his kiss was almost enough to bring her to her knees.

The first brush of his lips against hers was the most incredible thing she'd ever felt in her life. He kept the kisses light, fleeting, brushing at her mouth the way his cock brushed against her stomach, teasing her with what lay beneath both his lips and the leather. The hand caressing her ass was both possessive and gentle. She looked up at him, stunned at the ferocious desire he'd managed to pull from her with just a few touches. The desire stamped across his features brought her to her senses with a jolt.

What the hell am I doing? This is my boss!

With a gasp, she pulled away. "The dance is over." Turning on her heel, her cheeks heated with embarrassment, she practically ran off the dance floor and headed straight for the ladies' room.

She told herself it wasn't that she was *hiding* from Leo. After all, she had to do something about her wet panties or she was going to wind up staining her expensive leather skirt. Right?

Too bad I don't believe myself. She threw open the bathroom door and bolted inside like the little chicken she knew she was, grateful she hadn't broken her neck in her mad, stumbling, boots-from-hell dash across the room.

Chapter Two

What the hell is she doing?

Leo watched as his little imp left him standing in the middle of the dance floor. His cock was hard and aching and his mind totally confused. "Shit."

"Ruby's shy."

He turned towards Mandy, who was dancing with Dave from Marketing. Dave was currently dressed as a Viking, an easy choice with his blond good looks.

Leo cocked one eyebrow at Mandy and received a glare in return. "Seriously. She's shy. I had to double-dog dare her to wear that outfit. Do you think Little Miss Conservative would have worn it otherwise?"

His gaze traveled back to his little devil just in time to see her disappear into the ladies' room. *Oh, no you don't. No more running away.* He looked back at Mandy, winked, and sauntered after his devil, determined that this time she wouldn't avoid him.

Before he got two steps, his guardian angel grasped his arm. "By the way, she doesn't think she's attractive."

He turned, astonished, and stared at her in total disbelief. Ruby was one of the sexiest women he'd ever seen. She shrugged. "There's a history there, some stuff even I don't know about, but it's true. She thinks she's short and fat."

She thinks what? The image of her in that racy corset, and that seductive skirt, with those sexy boots...how could she think she was fat? She wasn't fat, she was *perfect*. He took a deep breath and let it out. "Thanks, Amanda. I appreciate all your help."

"No problem. But, just so you know, boss or no boss, you hurt her and I'll hire some really burly guys to rip your head off and shit down your neck."

She smirked and danced off in the arms of the Viking, leaving Leo with a bemused expression on his face. Turning back to the ladies' room, he stalked across the floor, dodging the social groups littering its edges. He side-stepped the rather blatant come-on of a slightly drunk redhead, hoping she was one of the employees taking advantage of the free rooms. With a wink and a shrug, he pointed to the ladies' room. She sighed wistfully and headed for the bar, leaving him standing in shadows.

Leo crossed his arms and waited for Ruby to come back to him. It had taken him weeks to put this plan into action. There was no way in hell he was letting her walk away from him tonight. Not until he knew for sure whether or not she was the one. But from the way his body and mind were reacting, he was pretty sure of the outcome. Now all he had to do was claim her. He grinned at the door, eager to confirm what every sense already told him was true.

Ruby didn't know whether it was possible to die of embarrassment or not. She was so flushed and hot from her erotic dance with her boss (her *boss* for Christ's sake!) that she was literally shaking.

"Hey, nice! We all wondered who would finally capture Leo's

attention." Suzanne, the accounting department's secretary, gave her a thumbs-up on entering the bathroom.

Ruby bit her lip. "I haven't captured his attention!"

Suzanne laughed. "Wanna bet? He's standing outside the ladies' room, and I doubt he's waiting for me!" With that she entered a stall.

Ruby sighed.

"Oh, by the way, he said you should come out, and he double-dog dares you."

Shit.

He was watching the door, waiting for Suzanne to deliver his message. Ruby popped her head out long enough to stick out her tongue, darting back in before he could grab a hold of her. She could hear him laughing through the closed doors.

He laughed. I stuck my tongue out at him like a ten-year-old, and he laughed.

"Aw, c'mon, Ruby!" She could hear the laughter in his voice, could almost picture the bad little boy smile that would be on his face. "Come dance with me again? Pleeease?"

Something inside her eased a bit. His laugh had been genuine, not the kind that hurt, but the kind that wanted you to share in it. She was tempted to peek back out but odds were good he'd be a little closer to the door this time. She wondered if she could just wait here until the party was over.

No. Way too juvenile. Besides, with the way he was acting, he might just come in and try to fetch her. Or worse, send in Mandy. With a sigh she straightened both her horns, and her spine, and drifted to the door.

"Good luck!" Suzanne stepped out of the stall with a smirk and headed for the sinks.

"Thanks," Ruby muttered, opening the door a crack and

peeking out. She'd barely got the door opened when a strong, masculine hand snaked in, grabbed her by the arm, and yanked her out. Pulling her behind him, Leo headed back to the dance floor. Wrapping her securely in his arms, he grinned down at her. "Gotcha."

"I thought you were supposed to be the devil, not a caveman," she grumbled, trying not to notice how good he smelled and failing miserably.

"I'm not Lucifer. I'm just a very horny guy."

Ruby stared up at him, her jaw dropping in shock. She didn't know whether to laugh or scream for help. "I can't believe you just said that." A wicked grin teased his lips. "Wait, scratch that. Yes I can."

He laughed, hugging her closer, his head bending over hers in a move that screamed possession. His hands roamed down her back, landed on her ass and squeezed. "Believe it," he whispered, rocking her closer to his aching erection.

He leaned down and kissed her. And not those light, butterfly kisses he'd given her earlier. Oh no. This time it seemed like he was intent on licking her toes through her mouth.

Shock raced through her system. *Oh my God, I'm being kissed by Leo Dunne! Either he's lost a bet, his mind, or...*

He plundered her mouth and she lost her train of thought, caught up in the heat and wonder of Leo's desire.

When his tongue darted between her lips to dance with hers she moaned, and it was all he could do to keep his hands steady. Little flickers of light danced behind his eyes, his magic almost pulling out of his control. Something clicked into place inside him. His veins bubbled with joy, tenderness towards the petite woman in his arms filling him to damn near overflowing.

Gods above, I knew it! She's the one! He pulled away from the kiss, breathing hard, mind reeling from the knowledge that he'd finally, *finally* found the one woman born to be his.

Ruby gulped, her face full of stunned heat. "Help?"

He leaned down quickly and licked the tender joining of her neck and shoulder. He felt her tremble under his hands. *Oh, a hot spot. I'll have to explore that later.* "Glad to." He heard the hint of Irish in his voice and couldn't care less. He had his woman in his arms and all was right with the world.

The slow music they'd been drifting to gave way to something a bit more energetic. Leo lifted his head and looked around the room for a tall, blonde angel. Finding Mandy occupied with her Viking, Leo decided to make his move. He took his little devil by the hand and pulled her towards the ballroom door.

"Where are we going?"

He could hear the nerves in her voice but when he glanced back her expression was amused. She clutched his hand, trying to keep her balance in those sexy-as-sin four-inch heels. When she tripped and righted herself he frowned, resisting the urge to just pick her up and carry her. He didn't think she'd go for that quite yet, although his inner caveman would be more than happy. "Somewhere private."

She yanked back hard on his hand, stopping him in his tracks. "Hold up there, buddy. I'm not sure this is such a good idea."

He turned and looked down at her, trying his best to look harmless. "I just want to talk, away from all the noise. Don't you want to get out of those boots for a bit without worrying about getting your toes stepped on?"

He saw the indecision on her face, the teasing light leaving her eyes. "You've got a certain reputation around the company,

Leo. Let's face it, I'm not exactly your type. Even if I was, I wouldn't want to be another notch on the old bedpost."

He actually felt his cheekbones heat up. He cleared his throat, trying to figure out how to get her to agree to leave the party with him. "If I promise not to touch you without your permission, will you come with me?"

She bit her lip, clearly undecided.

"I give you my word I won't do anything you don't want me to do." He held up one hand and pressed it against his heart, striking a theatrically wounded pose. "Don't you trust me?"

To his delight she lifted one skeptical eyebrow. He laughed, dropping the pose. "My word is gold, and you know it."

She narrowed her eyes at him. "Promise?"

"Promise." *That my word is gold, darlin'.* He caught a whiff of her wonderful scent and nearly groaned. His hand tightened around hers, daring her to make a break for it.

"Well, all right." She was frowning. He beamed angelically and pulled her along behind him, not giving her a chance to throw up any more obstacles.

Once out of the ballroom he headed straight for the elevators. "I'm not planning on staying the night," she muttered, biting her lip.

He wasn't surprised she'd said that, considering what she knew about his reputation. The fact that his reputation was mostly exaggerated didn't matter, only what she perceived it to be did. He'd have to figure out a way to fix that. "That's all right. I wasn't planning on it either." *Planning, no. Hoping, yes.*

She looked a little more relaxed, so he decided not to enlighten her.

They stepped into the elevator and he pressed the button for the penthouse, resisting the childish urge to punch the sky and shout *Yes!*

The penthouse was absolutely amazing, with gold-papered walls, rich, burgundy fabrics covering the sofa and chairs and a mahogany entertainment center. A small kitchenette was off to her left complete with a small table and two chairs. She assumed the bedroom was off to the right. The entire back wall of the room was made of glass, affording her an incredible view of the city below, all lit up for the night like the world's largest Christmas tree. The carpet beneath her poor, sore feet was soft and plush, a warm honey tone that complimented the walls.

With a deep sigh of satisfaction, Ruby plopped down on the sofa and considered taking her boots off. Leo watched her for a moment, looking uncertain, like she might just up and run away from him. When she reached down and began easing down the zipper on her boot, she could have sworn she heard a sigh of relief. She looked at him, curious, but he had his back to her and was busy pouring them both a drink. She took both boots and set them under the end table, wiggling her toes in the thick, decadent carpet with a quickly muffled moan. Damn it felt good to get those stupid boots off.

Leo handed her the glass of cola and sat on the coffee table in front of her. "I noticed at the last office party that you don't drink very much, so I thought you'd appreciate this."

She was surprised he'd noticed her or that he remembered. The last office party had been about six weeks ago, a retirement party for one of the IT guys. She'd done her best to stick to the shadows, avoiding anywhere Leo was. She hadn't wanted to make a fool of herself by drooling on him. Besides, he'd brought some blonde harpy with him. The woman had made faces all through the party, making it clear that she would much rather be somewhere alone with Leo.

Dare to Believe

Ruby was absurdly pleased he'd noticed despite his date's attempts to hold his attention. She saw he had the other half of the soda in his glass, and her smile turned to a grin. When he held the glass up in a silent toast, she tossed her hair back and clinked her glass to his before taking a sip.

"So, tell me about yourself." She tilted her head at him and he shrugged. "I know something about every single employee in the firm except you. You are a total enigma."

Ruby bit her lip and sighed. He was right. She'd gone out of her way to avoid him. "Let's see. I'm twenty-four, never been married, have a bachelor's degree from VSU, and, um, I live alone except for my cat, Cliona."

He choked on a mouthful of soda. "C-Cliona?"

She pounded him on the back. She didn't know many grown men who were willing to admit to liking fairy tales. "You like Irish fairy tales?"

She could sense he was struggling with a laugh and wondered at it. "You could say that. My parents are both Irish. Why did you name your cat after a fairy queen?"

"She's a cat, therefore she's a queen already." Ruby shrugged, wondering why she was slightly embarrassed. "I liked the name, and the legend."

"She ran away from Tir Nan Og with a mortal lover, only to have the fairies steal her back."

Ruby could feel herself blushing under Leo's intense scrutiny and turned her face away to stare at the glass in her hand. It was like he was trying to read her mind. "I think she should have been allowed to be with her lover. It wasn't fair of the faeries to decide he wasn't good enough for her." She pushed a lock of hair behind her ear and could have sworn she heard a soft groan. "Anyway, Cliona pretty much rules the place." She looked up at him out of the corner of her eye. "Do you have any pets?"

He nodded. "Actually, I have several. I have a cat named Clannad—"

"Like the band?"

He nodded. "I also have a dog named Eire, and horse named Mr. Ed."

It was her turn to choke on a sip of soda. "Mr. Ed?"

He shrugged, looking a little sheepish and a whole lot sexy. "He likes to talk back."

She laughed. "My parents are still together, and living in Petersburg. Yours?"

"Still very much in love. They have a farm out in Nebraska."

"You're a Nebraska farm boy?" She could hear the disbelief in her voice and bit her lip, hoping he wouldn't be offended and end one of the best nights she'd had in a long time.

One dark brow rose cockily. "Want to see me hitch a plow and dig a furrow?"

"Maybe later." She blushed again and turned her gaze back down to her glass. *Now what made me say that?*

She gave him big brownie points for holding back his laugh.

He sipped the soda in his glass before putting the glass down on the coffee table. He leaned forward, folding his hands and leaning his elbows on his knees. "My parents emigrated from Ireland after my father met and fell in love with my mother." She sensed rather than saw his shrug. "Funny, the way you feel about Cliona. My mom's family...well, let's say they're a little upper-crusty. They considered my father beneath them, so when my mom decided to marry him they threatened to disown her."

She looked into his eyes and saw no pain or regret there.

"Does your family see them at all?"

He sighed. "My grandparents passed away. The rest of the clan only sees us occasionally, and it's always a little awkward. Mom can't forget the way they treated Dad, but Dad doesn't hold a grudge. As far as he's concerned, they only wanted what was best for their daughter."

"He sounds like a good man."

"He is." There was a total conviction in his voice that betrayed the love and respect he had for his father. Ruby found herself revising her opinion slightly of her playboy boss. He sounded like someone whose family meant a great deal to him.

"Do you have any brothers or sisters?" Ruby had neither, but loved hearing about other's families.

"I have a younger sister, Moira, and an older brother, Shane."

"The middle child, huh? How did you wind up with Leo?"

He leaned back, his face full of laughter and memories. "Rock paper scissors."

"Huh?"

"My parents played rock paper scissors to figure out what to name us. Best two out of three won. Dad won twice, Mom won once."

"And you were Leo?"

"Yup. She said I roared like a lion from the day I was born."

She couldn't help it. She had to laugh.

"How'd your parents come to name you Ruby?"

"My mom's favorite soap opera character. She was so strong, and my mom wanted that for me. It's sort of a good luck charm."

There was a brief contemplative silence, each of them trying to think of what to say or ask next. It was strange in that it didn't feel awkward, the way such silences tended to be. There weren't that many people she felt comfortable with. Surprising that Leo Dunne seemed to be one of them.

"Are you hungry?"

Her stomach rumbled loudly at the thought of food.

"I'll take that as a yes." He grinned and handed her the room service menu. "Get whatever you want, it's on me."

"Thanks." *And what a buffet that would be!* Ruby shivered and looked down at the menu, trying not to picture how good he'd look coated in chocolate mousse.

The meal was excellent, the beef tender, the potatoes just right, the wine not too sweet. Leo made sure he ordered a desert with whipped cream, just to watch her lick it off the spoon with those luscious, full lips and pink tongue. This was the best first date he'd ever been on. She was relaxed and laughing, telling stories about his accounting department that normally would have caused his hair to stand on end.

Her eyes warmed to a delicious honey color when she was happy. He could stare into them for hours, and felt like he already had. He'd lit the candles on the table, trying to add a touch of romance to the meal. The light danced across her skin, creating intriguing shadows he was dying to explore. He could barely contain himself. He wanted to touch her so badly it actually hurt. His heart was thumping a mile a minute and his palms were sweating so badly he had to wipe them on his pants repeatedly. It was a wonder she didn't think him a total moron. He had no idea what he'd said to her all through dinner.

She was toying with her glass of wine, her expression soft and misty, the stories having finally run out. She reached up and pushed a lock of hair behind her ear, baring the side of her neck, and he opened his mouth, knowing something stupid would come out and wind up ending the best fucking night of his life.

"May I kiss you?"

He saw the way her breathing changed at his request, first hitching, then coming faster. It was all he could do not to yank her out of her chair and across his lap. Little sparkles of light leaped from his fingertips. He quickly pushed his hands under the table, hoping she hadn't noticed. He'd never wanted someone so badly that he'd been unable to control his powers before. "I promised I wouldn't touch you without your permission." The urge to put her in his bed, tie her up, and never let her go was so strong he was shaking with it. He clenched his fists in his lap, getting his magic back under control with a surge of his will.

When she licked her lips he nearly lost control again. "Yes."

The soft, nervous quality in her voice only added to her appeal. He wanted to take care of her, to let her know she would have nothing to fear, either from him or anyone else, ever again. He would protect her with everything he had, no matter the cost.

He stood up and held out his hand. She took his offer and let him help her to her feet. He led her over to the sofa and helped her sit down, much to her visible confusion. Apparently she'd been expecting him to kiss her standing up. He'd much rather be comfortable, and the sofa was plush and inviting, rather like the woman sitting on it. He sat down next to her and cupped her cheek in his hand. She leaned into his palm unconsciously, a move that spoke of a trust he hadn't yet earned, but was determined to prove was not misplaced. Very slowly he leaned forward and placed his lips over hers.

She tasted like chocolate and wine, sweet and rich, with

that underlying hint of woman that drove him nearly insane. He couldn't wait to see what the rest of her tasted like. The air was filled with her scent, making his head spin with need. He placed his hands on her shoulders and held her in place while he began a leisurely exploration of her mouth that had them both gasping for breath.

Ruby felt her breasts lift up in a silent plea for his hands. His kiss was easily the most erotic thing she'd ever felt in her entire life. She leaned into him, raising her hands to stroke his bare chest. His skin felt incredible, hot silk over hard muscles, a light smattering of hair around his dark brown nipples narrowing down to disappear into his tight leather pants. She'd been watching his naked chest all during dinner, dying to get her hands on it, and now she indulged herself, sliding them up and down, her fingers clenching slightly in pleasure at the incredible feel of him. She was rewarded for her efforts by his shudder.

Oh, yeah, let my fingers do the walking!

His kiss became hungrier, one of his hands moving up to her hair, his fingers twining in it to grasp the back of her head and tilt it. He began to ravish her mouth, his tongue thrusting in and out in a promise of what he wanted to do to her. Just tipsy enough to go with the flow, but not so tipsy she didn't know exactly what she was about to do, she drew her hands down his chest until her fingers lightly brushed his nipples. She played with them to her heart's content, tweaking them into hard little points, her reward the groan he couldn't hold back.

When he pushed her back against the arm of the sofa she went willingly, her panties already soaked through with her juices. He kept one hand buried in her hair, holding her in place. With the other he eased down the front of the red satin corset to reveal her breasts to the cool air of the room. His actions were slow enough that she could have stopped him at any moment, but she had no desire to. Her nipples, already hard and aching, brushed against his chest, sending jolts of pleasure straight to her clit. Unconsciously she began to move her hips up against him, silently pleading for his hands, his tongue, any touch he was willing to give her. She'd never felt this kind of fire for a man before. Its strength was frightening, but the thought of pulling away was even scarier.

Breaking from the kiss, he began nibbling his way down, lingering in the sensitive juncture of her neck and shoulder until she was shuddering with need. One of her hands went up to the back of his head and held him to her. He licked and sucked, his teeth scraping along her skin before latching on. From the strong suction of his mouth she just knew he was leaving his mark on her. She arched into him, sucking on her bottom lip at the incredible sensations shooting from his mouth straight to her nipples and clit.

Abruptly he sat up, his breathing harsh in the silence of the room. "Damn, Ruby. Better tell me now if you want me to stop or not. I'm about to hit the point of no return, here."

She watched his throat move as he swallowed convulsively. She could see how affected he was. He sucked in deep breaths, staring at her naked breasts, hunger and something more written all over his face. When he licked his lips she hissed, her body arching slightly towards his in a subconscious plea for more. She'd never felt like this before, like she would die if she didn't have him *right now.*

He clenched his fists at his sides to keep from touching her, his legs straddling her thighs, quivering with obvious need held firmly in check. "Choose."

She could see the strain not touching her put on him. He

held himself steady, watching her, his whole body tight with need. He trembled, waiting for her answer, and she knew if she denied him he'd let her go. It would probably kill them both in the process, but he'd do it.

It said a lot about him that he'd kept his word that he wouldn't touch her without her permission.

She looked up at him through eyes gone heavy with lust and threw seven years of caution to the winds. *When am I ever going to have a chance like this again?* Men like Leo didn't usually go for women like her, but for tonight, there was no doubt in her mind that he did. "Do it."

One brow arched. "Do what, Ruby?"

She licked her lips, suddenly nervous. "Do *me*."

Emotion flashed across his face, gone too quickly for her to see what it was. Surprise, maybe? Pleasure glittered there now, mixing in with the lust. "Do what to you, Ruby?" The slightest hint of a brogue only increased his incredible sexiness. One hand reached down to tweak her nipple. The other hand began a lazy massage of his cock behind his zipper. Her eyes were drawn to the sight almost unwillingly before they turned towards his.

"Make love to me." She looked up at him, her voice pleading and heavy with desire. "Please."

"My pleasure."

Chapter Three

Leo nearly came in his pants. It took all of his self control to stop the magic from getting away from him. If she looked anywhere but at him she'd probably see little fireflies of light darting around the room, something that hadn't happened to him before. He'd *never* lost it this badly. There was a catch in her voice, a plea he'd rarely heard, the cry of a woman who didn't think she was pleasing but wanting something she couldn't name.

Leo decided that from now on he'd see to it that she never doubted her appeal again.

With that in mind, he moved the hand fondling his cock down to her skirt. With a wicked grin on his face he began inching it up, exposing the thigh-high stockings and red thong panties she wore to his admiring gaze.

"Damn, kitten. I like your taste in underwear." He petted her covered mound, earning a hiss of pleasure. He turned his hand and cupped her, easing the fabric aside enough to allow his fingers to stroke through her drenched slit. He looked down and shuddered with need.

She was completely bald. "So fucking sexy." He couldn't wait to see her uncovered, but first he wanted to see her come. He strummed her clit, watching her reactions closely, trying to see what made her crazy with want. She arched into his hand with a soft cry, her breath hitching. "Right there, kitten?"

He cupped her breast with his free hand, stroking the soft skin around her areola before moving to the brown nipple. His fingers stroked in circles to match the rhythm he was using on her clit. "Beautiful. So fucking beautiful."

She hunched up against him, her hands stroking his chest, her eyes closed in pleasure. He began to stroke her to climax, dying to see her face in ecstasy.

"Please. God, please!" she pleaded breathlessly.

He leaned down and took one pebbled nipple into his mouth. He sucked and licked as hard as he dared. He slipped two of his fingers into her hot, wet sheath, matching the tugging pull of his mouth to the stroking of his fingers. He kept his gaze on her face, gauging her reactions by the expressions flitting across it. From what he could see it wouldn't be much longer before she tumbled over the edge.

He bit down, letting her just feel the edge of his teeth. She came with a cry, her muscles clenching down over his fingers like a vise. Before she finished, he eased down her panties and sucked her clit into his mouth, prolonging her orgasm.

She came down from the orgasm, her breathing ragged. He moved from sucking her clit to licking her slit, trying to ease her down without losing that little touch of arousal he planned on using to go even further. "God, that was so good." There was a note of surprise in her voice.

He laughed, happy that he'd pleased her. He spared a brief thought to the lovers she'd had who'd failed to, but decided the losers weren't worth more than that. After all, it was their loss and very much his gain. "Don't worry, kitten, the night's young. It'll get much, much better."

"Much better than that, and you're going to be explaining my death-by-orgasm to the county coroner."

The breathless laughter in her voice warmed him. He rewarded her with another long, slow lick.

"Oh. Oh, my. Leo, what are you doing?"

"Eating you, my dear," he breathed against her wet, inflamed flesh. He couldn't help himself. It was the sweetest looking pussy he'd ever seen. He nibbled at her clit and she rewarded him with a breathless moan.

"*Oh.* Okay."

Leo held back another laugh. He'd never had a lover who made him want to laugh in bed before. He found that he loved that about her. He began to tongue her clit, lapping at it like a cat at a bowl of cream. He inserted two fingers into her and began languidly thrusting them in and out. Her thighs quivered. Looking up at her over her bare mound he saw her playing with her nipples, bringing them to hard peaks once more. His cock became rock hard behind his tight leather pants at the sight of her enjoying her body.

If he didn't fuck her soon he was going to explode.

She was moaning and panting with need, her body arching against the burgundy velvet of the couch, her gorgeous tits cupped in her hands. She began to ride the wave towards another orgasm, her expression exquisitely painful. "Please, please, please," she muttered breathlessly.

"Say my name," he whispered, lapping at her pussy.

"Leo."

"Again." He took her clit between his lips and hummed, using just enough of his magic to send the vibrations skyrocketing through her.

"*Leo!*" She came on a scream, his name ringing out through the hotel room, her body bowed up off the sofa, her arms flying up above her head, fingers digging into the cushions. One of his hands grasped her hip, keeping her from throwing them both off the sofa with the force of her orgasm.

She whimpered, coming down from what sounded like one hell of an orgasm. He continued to lap at her, removing his fingers from her to tug at the zipper of his leather pants, so damn hard he hurt.

She opened dazed eyes and looked down at him. His tongue reached out and touched her soaking wet slit and she shivered in response. His hot gaze meeting hers, his hand moved down to his pants. She imagined him lowering the zipper one set of teeth at a time. She tried to sit up, only to have him hold her down.

"Stay there." His command was dark and ragged. He stood and pulled his rock hard cock out of his pants, stroking it lightly. She couldn't take her eyes off it. He slid one leg over her to partially kneel on the sofa over her chest, one foot on the floor keeping him steady. He held the purple head to her lips, a demanding expression on his face. He stayed perfectly still, waiting to see what she'd do.

Ruby had never given anyone a blow job before, but after giving her two mind-blowing orgasms with his tongue and lips, she figured she owed him one. Besides, how hard could it be? She was intelligent. She'd read some really steamy novels. She knew the mechanics.

Remembering some things Mandy had told her and others she'd read, she licked gently at the head of his cock, breathing in his musky, male scent. The drop of liquid at the tip was both salty and sweet, and he groaned when she delicately lapped it up. She felt her body coming to life once again, her nipples standing at attention. He reached down and toyed with one, sending sharp pleasure straight to her pussy. His other hand moved into her hair to hold her head steady. She opened her lips and he slipped the head of his cock inside, the warm weight strange on her tongue.

She sucked on it, pleased when he sighed his pleasure. Looking up at him through her lashes, she could see his eyes glued to her mouth. Leo began moving his cock between her lips, keeping her head where he wanted it with his hand.

She stroked the shaft with her tongue, earning a groan from him. He closed his eyes, the fingers in her hair becoming firmer around the back of her head. Heat curled in her stomach at his firm grip, surprising her. He began carefully moving her head back and forth, his hips hunching to meet her mouth.

"Gods, baby, that's it. Lick it, kitten. Use your tongue."

She obeyed his soft command, stroking his cock with her tongue. When she hollowed out her cheeks and sucked down hard, he pulled out of her mouth with a hiss. "Not yet, kitten. I don't want to come in your mouth."

"Didn't you say the night was young?" Her own daring surprised her.

He stared down at her, surprised and pleased. "Yeah. Yeah, I did, didn't I?" He guided the head of his cock back between her lips. "Suck it, kitten. Make me come."

He began moving more forcefully between her lips, his eyes never leaving the sight of his cock entering and leaving her mouth. "That's it, kitten. Gods, that's good. I'm going to come soon."

She could taste him now, that salty sweet flavor stronger than before, and wondered if he was close. His breathing sped up, his hips hunched faster against her, and with a groan he erupted into her mouth, flooding her with his taste. She wasn't prepared for it. She tried her best to swallow but nearly choked, some of it getting away from her and dribbling out of her mouth. She liked the look on his face as he came. He continued to stare down at her, his face twisted in helpless ecstasy. She kept sucking him even after he was done and was rewarded with a happy, satisfied laugh. He pulled her head away from his half-erect cock. He replaced his cock with his tongue in a kiss that was both tender and possessive, surprising her. She didn't think he'd want to kiss her after he'd come in her mouth, but from the warmth of it she guessed he didn't mind. He stroked her hair throughout the kiss and her arms crept around his neck, her heart stuttering strangely in her chest. In a way it was even more intimate than the sex had been.

He picked her up off the sofa and swung her up into his arms as if she weighed nothing at all. "Time to get naked, kitten."

He turned on his heel and carried her into the bedroom.

Once inside the burgundy and cream bedroom he set her on her feet. He peeled the red corset off her, savoring each bit of exposed skin, kissing and nibbling at her in seemingly random spots until she was ready to beg him to lick her nipples. He went to his knees in front of her and unzipped her red leather mini skirt. He slid it down her legs to the floor. She stepped out of the skirt, now clad in only the thigh-high stockings. His fingers glided over the smooth nylons soothingly, touching every inch of her silk-encased legs, until he glided up to the juncture of her thighs. With a wild groan he buried his face in her pussy, licking her clit almost frantically.

With a surprised cry, she came, writhing in his grasp. His hands closed firmly around the globes of her ass, holding her in place, letting her ride it out, keeping her safe. When it was over he stood up and hauled her into his arms, kissing her ruthlessly. Their two flavors combined on her tongue, making her almost wild with want. She pulled away from the kiss. "Fuck me, Leo."

Leo looked down into her wild eyes and groaned. She pulled out of his arms and fell to her knees with a hungry look. She eased his pants down his legs and pressed a gentle kiss to his hard cock. Her soft hands drove him insane with butterfly touches to his ass, his balls, even the back of his knees. His cock sprang to full attention, eager for more. She unbuckled his boots, pulling them off his feet and practically flinging them away. He finished removing his pants, dying to see what his kitten was going to do next.

She took his cock in her hands and began to pump. She moved up and down the shaft, pulling on the upstroke so that his balls bounced back and forth. She licked the purple head, sucking at it till a drop of precome oozed out of the tip.

"*Shit,*" he hissed, trying desperately not to come again in her greedy little mouth, astonished at how fierce the desire was this time, especially considering the explosive orgasms they'd already had.

He reached down to pull her to her feet. She went willingly, laughing when he picked her up and tossed her onto the bed with a low, throaty growl. Leo stalked over to the bed and began crawling up her body, pausing only long enough to suckle at her nipples until she was wet and writhing beneath him. Little mews of pleasure were pouring from her lips now, red and swollen from his kisses, her expression part pleasure, part pain. He nipped at the hard pebbles of her nipples with his teeth, almost coming right then when her head arched back, exposing the long line of her neck. The move was inherently submissive, showing her trust in him. He felt like a fucking caveman claiming his woman. He went to his knees above her, pulled her knees apart and settled himself between them. "Got to fuck you now," he muttered roughly, shocking her dazed eyes open. He bent to her in a savage kiss that took the breath from both of them.

"Leo." She was gasping when he released her lips, her expression half-dazed fear, half-crazed desire. He'd never seen anything more alluring in his entire life. Her hands were on his hips, tugging him into her. Her nails were digging into him, marking his flesh.

He took both of her thighs into his hands and fitted himself to her tight sheath. With a low, guttural cry he pushed into her, filling her, his balls landing against her ass.

Mine.

He'd never, in his entire long life, felt anything as incredible as the wet sheath now surrounding him. A part of him watched her reactions, noticed when her body relaxed into his, and waited. It was almost like she was a virgin, but no virgin could have given him such ecstasy. He breathed deep, expanding his senses to the utmost. No, no scent of virgin's blood, no hint in her mind that this was her first time. Maybe it had been a while for her. He throbbed inside her, desperately trying to hold back while she adjusted to his size.

Hell, it had been a while for him, too, all rumors to the contrary. Since he'd seen a certain perfect ass bent over a desk, to be exact.

When she finally opened her eyes and looked up at him, he smiled down at her, trying to reassure her while his body clamored for him to start thrusting *now*. When she licked her lips he nearly lost it.

"Okay now?" He could hear the plea in his voice. If she didn't give him the okay soon, he'd start whimpering and blow his macho right out the window.

She nodded. With a whispered, reverent *thank you*, he began to thrust himself in and out of her warm, wet body.

Ruby felt like she'd been impaled on a tree trunk. He was

much, *much* bigger than Bobby What's-His-Face had been. If she'd known that calling Bobby "Pencil Dick" was really *accurate*...

She began moving her hips in time with his thrusts, the movement brushing her clit against the base of his cock. That sent sensations rocketing through her body that she really, really liked, so she started to speed up. When he groaned, she looked up at him.

His head was thrown back, his eyes closed, his face a grimace of passion. He eased in and out of her carefully, like he was afraid of hurting her. He *had* to be holding back.

Screw that. This was the first time she'd had sex in seven long years, and it was with *Leo Dunne*. No way was she going to let him take it easy on her!

She reached up her hands, gliding them over the smooth muscles of his chest. She just couldn't seem to get enough of the sculpted planes and angles. He thrust in and out of her body with ease. The feel of him moving above her with primal grace made her want to touch, to taste every single inch of him while he writhed in her grasp. When she reached his stomach he jerked and pushed more of himself into her, causing her to gasp with pleasure.

She reached behind him and grabbed the firm globes of his ass, watching his cock shuttled in and out of her body intently. The sight was fascinating, something she'd never thought she'd see even in her wildest dreams. She pulled at him, trying to get more of him inside. "Easy, kitten. You're really tight. How long has it been?"

"Seven years," she muttered, tugging at his ass cheeks again.

She whimpered when he stopped. "Seven *years*?"

"Leo!" She hated whining, but damn it, some situations

called for it. This was definitely one of them.

She sighed in relief when he started moving again, thrusting in and out of her harder now, as if the fact she hadn't gotten laid in seven years was a turn-on for him. With a sigh of satisfaction she felt him seat himself fully into her for the first time. She closed her eyes, savoring the sensation of his thick, hard cock moving inside her with increasing speed.

Leo could hear it whispering in his head in time with his thrusts: *Mine!* He hadn't felt this good since… Hell. Nothing had *ever* been *this* good.

He could feel his magic wrapping itself around them, a glittering, sparkling curtain he could do nothing about. It was hard enough not spilling his seed into her waiting body before she was ready for it. There was no way he could control his powers.

His magic scented the air with vanilla and peaches, causing her to smile. That soft expression nearly finished him, so sweet and sexy, a smile he vowed then and there no other man would ever see. That particular look was *his*.

He began pulling on her body, faster and faster, thrusting himself in and out of her with growing urgency. The lights surrounding them began to glow brighter and brighter, his climax inching closer. He could tell from the way she moved and moaned beneath him that she was about to explode. He had to make sure she came first. He needed their first time together to be perfect for her.

He wouldn't be able to hold out much longer. Her eyes were still tightly shut, her teeth nibbling at her lip as she strained up against him. Her brow furrowed, her lip curled, and he knew she was almost there. He reached between them and flicked her clit hoping to push her over that final edge.

She came screaming, flinging herself at him, pulling him into her so tightly that when he came his whole body pulsed with light and the room around them lit up like the fourth of July. He could feel himself throbbing inside her, the pleasure nearly blinding him, his come bathing her womb, his light bathing her skin, Claiming her, marking her as his.

He collapsed against her, half dead from the best goddamned sex he'd ever had in his life, and wondered how quickly he could talk her into bonding.

Ruby floated down from somewhere so high she hadn't been able to breathe. There was a heavy, warm weight draped over her. She could feel someone breathing heavily next to her ear. She opened her eyes.

Leo was draped over her, his arms clutching her to him tightly like he was afraid she was going to get up and run from the bed. Her thighs were still cradling his, his now soft cock just beginning to slide from her body.

Maybe she really *had* stopped breathing. She could swear she saw fading, twinkling lights surrounding them. A sure sign of oxygen deprivation.

She giggled.

Leo stirred against her, the curve of his lips tickling the side of her neck. He lifted himself to look down at her. "Mind letting me in on the joke?"

"I think I was oxygen deprived."

He tilted his head, a question in his gaze.

"I actually saw little lights a minute ago, like you do when you're mountain climbing and the air is really thin."

He frowned, concerned. "You've actually experienced that?"

She giggled again. "Discovery Channel."

He rolled over onto his side with a sigh, gathering her limp, sated body against his. He kissed her forehead tenderly, and she shivered, startled.

"I don't know about you but I'm exhausted. Go to sleep, Ruby."

"Oh, but—"

"No buts, kitten." He lifted his head and looked down at her, a mixture of tenderness and command on his face. "Go to sleep."

She licked her lips. Suddenly, things seemed a little more intense than she'd planned on. "I wasn't planning on staying the night."

"I wasn't planning on making love to you tonight, either." Suddenly serious, he said, "Stay with me." Her breath caught in her throat at his expression. "Don't leave me before morning." Before she could reply, he leaned down and kissed her with a tenderness that left her breathless. "Please."

She only hesitated a moment. With a soft sigh she cuddled up against him, burying her face in his chest. Closing her eyes she willed her body to sleep. It didn't take long for the combination of wine, warmth and incredible sex to gently lull her to sleep.

She didn't see the relief that crossed his face or the tenderness as he watched her sleeping in his arms.

"Mine."

Jaden Blackthorn strolled down the hallway, looking neither left nor right. He'd been summoned here before, and he didn't like it one little bit.

Snagging the hybrid hadn't been easy, but he'd known it wouldn't be. He'd been strong, absurdly so, and that unique power of his had made things a little…touchy…at one point, but he'd pulled off the job.

Now the Deranged Darling wanted something more from him. Hell, at this point he was considering paying her room and board since she had him practically living in the mansion. The only thing that made it bearable was her fashionable Rodeo Drive ass was stuck in East Bumblefuck, Nebraska.

He desperately wished the Malmayne house was a ranch. He'd love to see her get cow shit all over her Pradas.

He reached the doorway at the end of the hall and pushed it open. He was singularly unimpressed by the rich surroundings of cherry wood, velvets and silks. Nothing here meant a damn to him other than it proved they could afford to pay him. This house belonged to Lord Cullen Malmayne and was as cold as the man himself. The home Jaden shared with Duncan was a great deal warmer.

Then again, an iceberg was warmer than this place. He couldn't wait to get out of here and go home.

Malmayne the elder was speaking to his daughter, trying once again to get her crazy ass to see reason. Jaden held back his sigh and waited.

"Shane is here and could easily fulfill the contract, Kaitlynn."

"I don't want Shane. I want Leo," a husky, feminine voice pouted.

If it wasn't for the fact that the voice belonged to one of the most spoiled women Jaden had ever met it would have sent shivers of lust down his spine. Instead he shuddered and turned to look at the tall, elegant blonde. Her white gold hair was done up in a simple French twist a la Grace Kelly. She'd worn a pale shade of pink today, complementing her fair skin, the silky material clinging to her understated curves. High heels in a matching shade were strapped on her dainty feet, emphasizing the long length of her legs. Gray eyes stared at her father with a forlorn expression, her luscious mouth tilted down at the edges.

Jaden hid another shudder. That mouth held teeth sharper than his, and that was saying something.

Malmayne the elder sighed. "I will see if we can negotiate with Leo, my dear, but he's turned down all other overtures. Perhaps, if Leo refuses, we should reconsider Shane?"

Jaden tuned them out, waiting silently and with the stillness only those of his kind could accomplish. He'd heard this argument before, and knew Cullen Malmayne would once again lose. He opened his senses to the surrounding area, listening to the heartbeats of all those around him, counting them out until he'd found even the two "hidden" guards Malmayne the elder thought protected him. Jaden hid his knowledge of the watchers, keeping his face bored.

"Mr. Blackthorn. Thank you for coming."

Jaden blinked and turned his darkest, most penetrating stare towards the blonde. "Ms. Malmayne."

He nearly allowed his grin to escape at her moue of distaste. "Would you like to have a seat, Mr. Blackthorn?"

"No, thank you, Ms. Malmayne. I prefer to stand."

There was a moment of confusion on her face before she blinked and gave him her false, sweet smile. "Mr. Blackthorn, I have another job for you."

Jaden nodded. "I kind of figured, hon, otherwise you wouldn't have called." He smirked, allowing his teeth to flash at her.

Dare to Believe

He watched her back straighten with outrage before she shook it off. Her expression was saccharine sweet. *Crap. Now what? Last time she looked like that she had me kidnap someone.* She handed him a piece of paper. "I want you to make the ransom demand on the Dunne family."

Jaden's smirk faded into a snarl he quickly wiped off his face. He took the piece of paper reluctantly. The whole set-up stunk to high heaven and he was already beginning to regret taking orders from the high-brow bitch. Hell, if Duncan had been home...

But Duncan *wasn't* home, and Cullen, the old sap, couldn't deny his daughter anything she wanted. Clothes, cars, jewelry. People.

And they had the balls to call *him* a vampire. It made an honest-to-god bloodsucker cringe.

With a sigh Jaden turned to find a phone.

"Don't call from here, you idiot! Find some anonymous phone."

Jaden turned back, his eyes flashing red with his irritation. "How about I go down to the local Wal-Mart and use the payphone there, sweet cheeks? Got a calling card I could use?"

"Don't call me that!" Jaden *loved* that rasping note of irritation in her voice. It took that smooth, sweet voice of hers and turned it into a verbal Brillo pad. "Do as I tell you or I'll let Jeremy West know what your weakness is. Doesn't he have a rowan tree on his property?"

Jaden paled. "You *bitch*." If Jeremy found his weakness, Jaden was a goner. And until he could figure out how to shut her mouth permanently he had to do what she said. If only Duncan would pick up his damn messages.

"I know." She stared down at her perfect manicure, that sweet, sweet smile on her face, and Jaden had to forcibly keep

51

his hands to himself. "It would be a shame if Jeremy found out how to destroy you completely, wouldn't it?"

With a growl, he glided out of the room and shut the door in her pampered face.

I hate that bitch. He looked down at the number on the paper and headed straight for her private room, misting through the lock easily. He picked up her private phone and placed the call he'd been ordered to make, all the while wishing Duncan would get back *soon*.

There was a freight train running outside her room. Which was odd, since her apartment wasn't anywhere near train tracks. Ruby groaned and pulled a pillow over her head.

Or tried to, anyway. Something else was on the pillow. "Get off, Cliona," she muttered, batting her hand at her cat.

There was a snort, followed by "ow" in a deep masculine voice.

Ruby's eyes flew open. Staring at her and holding his nose was Leo.

"Um." The events of the night before rushed through her head, bringing heat to her cheeks. "Good morning."

"Good morning." If she hadn't seen the happiness beginning to flirt around his mouth she would have been mortified. As it was, she was merely horribly embarrassed.

"Did I hurt you?" She reached out with one hand and stroked the bridge of his nose.

He took her hand in his and kissed her palm, heat, humor and tenderness making his eyes shine in the morning light. They even looked a different color, startlingly light and bright. "I'm fine, kitten." With a groan he rolled over and stretched, a

Dare to Believe

whole body stretch that involved flinging his arms over his head, his incredible chest bowing up off the bed. She bet if she looked under the covers she would see his toes curling. And he called *her* kitten. Right now, he reminded her of a sleek jungle cat, all muscle and sinew and *man*.

"How about a shower before breakfast?"

She blinked, staring. He climbed out of bed, his body magnificent in the early morning light. That golden color obviously wasn't a tan, either. There wasn't a single tan line on him. She knew; she looked. Closely.

"Of course, there are other things we can do before breakfast."

He caught her staring at his tight, firm ass. His low, sexy growl sent heat racing through her system. Oh yeah. She could go for some more of that.

Her stomach, however, had other plans. It growled, loudly. "Or not," he laughed, reaching down for her. He grasped her hand he pulled her from the bed. "C'mon, shower, then breakfast."

Before they could make it into the bathroom she heard the theme song from *The X-Files* coming from Leo's leather pants.

Leo picked up his pants and pulled out his cell phone. "Hey, Dad, what's up?"

Ruby held back a laugh. *The X-Files? Not what I'd pick for my dad.*

The expression on Leo's face slowly changed from happy to shocked. Her grin faded away, her concern for her new lover overriding all of the good feelings she'd woken up with. "When?" He stared at her and held out his hand. She took it and winced at the way his fingers curled tight around hers. "I'm on my way," he whispered, closing the phone. He clenched it in his fist, still staring at her blankly.

"Leo? What's wrong?"

He blinked and took a deep breath. He looked…devastated. "Shane."

She pulled on one of the courtesy robes, belting it around her waist. She stared at him, knowing this was the end of their idyllic morning after. "Your brother?"

He just stood there, his face building to a burning rage, and she knew something terrible had happened.

"He's been kidnapped."

Ruby looked out the window of the plane once again and wondered how the hell she'd let herself be talked into this.

He'd stared at her for a moment longer, naked, vulnerable, and hurting, and she hadn't been able to help herself. She'd gone to him, allowed him to cling to her, his big body shaking with rage and grief.

That vulnerability hadn't lasted long. Soon he was on the phone, arranging for the flight, asking that she order breakfast for the both of them while he made arrangements to go to his family.

She'd quickly showered while he paced, knowing he'd need to leave as soon as possible and he'd need the shower before he left. She'd dressed in the red skirt and corset, feeling even more out of place in it than she had at the party.

He'd taken the quickest shower she'd ever seen anyone take in her life, then pulled on the black leather pants and boots he'd worn the night before, minus the horns. He was on the phone all through breakfast, his face hard, his expression harsh and cold. He dealt with delegating some of his responsibilities in the office, letting his staff know that he'd be

Dare to Believe

on an extended leave of absence. It was obvious he had no intention of returning until his brother was found. A small part of her mourned that, but the larger part agreed with him.

By the time he was done he must have been starving. His stomach was growling so loudly she was surprised his staff couldn't hear it through the receiver. She reached for the phone to call a taxi to take her home, not wanting to burden him with anything at such a bad time. "Hello? I need a taxi at—"

She was startled when she found the receiver snatched out of her hands. "Never mind, the lady won't need that ride." He hung up the phone and stared at her, daring her to say something.

She licked her lips and, for just a second, saw his eyes heat up. "Leo, you don't need to be worrying about me right now." She put her hand on his arm, gazing up at him in concern. "You need to worry about your family. I can see myself home."

"I've made arrangements for a limo to stop off and pick us both up. We'll stop at my place first, I'll pack, and then we'll head to your place. Our plane leaves in four hours."

Her mouth opened but nothing came out. He reached up and pushed her jaw shut with one finger, his expression filled with ruthless determination. "Leo. What do you mean, 'our' plane?" She was proud of the fact that her voice wasn't shaking.

"You're going with me to Nebraska."

"I'm going home to my apartment, changing clothes and doing laundry. *You're* going to Nebraska."

"Don't fight me on this, Ruby." His voice matched his face, hard and uncompromising.

"You can't just up and take me to Nebraska, Leo! A, it's a federal crime to kidnap somebody, because I said no. B, it doesn't matter, because I said *no*. Besides, what about Cliona?" Her hands went to her hips, her toe tapping on the thick, soft carpet. Sort of like it wanted to tap on his thick, soft head.

"Taken care of. Mandy's agreed to watch out for her."

Ruby's jaw dropped again, this time in anger. "What?"

"Your bags should be packed by the time we get there. Mandy has been very helpful."

"You had no right!" He'd rearranged her life without even consulting her. *Well, at least I don't have to call my boss and tell him I won't be in tomorrow.*

He didn't pretend not to understand her. "I had every right."

"Leo—" she protested, only to be cut off when he put his fingers over her mouth.

His jaw clenched, pain leaking through the determination on his face. "I need you with me. Don't ask me any more questions than that. I can't explain it yet. Just... I need you to trust me. Please. I need *you.*"

And that, she knew, was what had done it. Strong, arrogant Leo Dunne had practically begged for her support. So here she was, winging her way to Nebraska, of all places, to stand by Leo's side and help him through this.

I'm an idiot. An idiot on a plane.

His head was back against the seat, his eyes closed, but she knew from the way his fingers were clamped around her hand that he was far from asleep. His thumb occasionally stroked hers. She couldn't tell if he was trying to soothe her or himself. She could feel from the tension in his body that he was far from calm, and wondered why it was that he wanted her with him so badly. She sighed deeply, squeezed his hand, and turned back towards the window, hoping she would be able to be what he needed.

Leo stroked Ruby's hand and tried desperately to stay calm despite the fear eating a hole in his stomach.

He couldn't believe she'd agreed to come, but was eternally grateful he hadn't had to force the issue. If necessary he would have used his magic to get her on board this plane, and damn the consequences.

To hell with the office. To hell with protocol. He *needed* her with him. He'd explain everything once they were on the farm.

No way was he letting her out of his sight. Thanks to him and the Claiming, she was in danger and didn't even know it.

His brother might be the victim, but he had the feeling he was the ransom.

Chapter Four

Ruby was once again staring out a window, but this time it was the window of the Lincoln Navigator Leo had picked up at the airport. "Have your parents heard anything from the kidnappers yet?"

Leo glanced at her, then turned his attention back to the road. "No, not yet. Other than the initial phone call letting them know he'd been taken, they haven't heard a thing."

"Do they know why he was taken?"

"It could be a number of reasons. First, they might know he's my brother, and I'd pay anything to get him back." His hands tightened on the wheel. "It could also have to do with Mom's family. There are those who still haven't accepted my parents' marriage."

She stared at him, stunned. "You're kidding me. After all these years?"

His smile was sour. "Let's just say they have long memories."

She whistled, not surprised when he turned his attention back to his driving. He was silent the entire way to the farm, his hands occasionally clenching the steering wheel. From the expression on his face she'd bet anything he was picturing his brother's kidnappers.

Dare to Believe

She stayed silent for the rest of the ride, eventually nodding off with her head against the window.

It was dark when Leo finally pulled into his father's farm. All of the lights were on in the old Victorian house, but that didn't surprise him. When he'd told his family he was bringing someone with him, he'd known they would be more than curious. He'd never brought a woman home with him before. And even if he had, he'd never bring an ordinary woman home with him under the current circumstances.

He pulled the truck to a stop in front of his parents' home, not surprised that there were no cars other than ones belonging to the immediate family there. He turned off the ignition and turned in his seat to face Ruby.

She was just beginning to wake up, staring around at, to her, unfamiliar surroundings. He watched her react to the farmhouse, her eyes going wide at the sight of the large Victorian home. "We're here." His voice was husky with fatigue.

She turned to him, looking oh so weary. "It's all right, Leo. They'll find him."

Her comfort warmed the cold place that had settled in around the pit of his stomach. When she placed one small hand against his cheek, he knew that if he hadn't already started to fall in love with her he'd have lost his heart then and there. He turned his face into her palm and kissed it, accepting the comfort she was offering. "Thank you."

She didn't question what he was thanking her for. She just waited in the car while he came around to help her out with a sleepy smile that went straight to his heart.

"Leo."

He turned to find his father standing on the porch, staring down at him with his hands on his hips, the porch light gleaming off his midnight dark hair. Blue eyes the color of a summer sky frowned down at him. "Get her inside. It's cold out here."

That Irish brogue, sure and steady, washed through him, calming him just as it had when he'd been a child.

His father turned to Ruby, smiling a warm yet sad welcome. "Welcome to my home."

His home? I thought Leo's parents still owned the farm? Ruby watched the man, who looked to be no more than a few years older than Leo, walk down the porch steps. His long, determined stride reminded her vividly of the way Leo moved. The man walked up to them, and Leo put his arm around her shoulders and hugged her close to the warmth of his big body.

She was pulled up short when the man clasped his hand around Leo's arm. "Welcome home, son." His voice held the lilt of Ireland in it, full of warmth that had been missing briefly when he'd first appeared on the porch.

Leo turned to the other man, and suddenly the two were embracing. "Wish the homecoming was under better circumstances, Dad."

Wait. Dad?

That dark haired, walking sex advertisement was Leo's *dad?*

"Dad, I'd like you to meet Ruby Halloway. Ruby, this is Sean Dunne."

The man lifted her hand to his lips and kissed her knuckles. "Welcome, Miss Halloway. I wish we'd met under better circumstances."

"Thank you, Mr. Dunne. I'm so sorry about your son."

Leo's father nodded, his expression shadowed. "Thank

you." He turned to Leo, the shadows disappearing. "Take your woman inside and introduce her properly to your mother. She's waiting on you." The man took the keys from Leo and walked to the trunk of the SUV. He turned and winked at her, popped the trunk open and began to remove their bags.

"C'mon, Ruby. Let's go introduce you to my mother."

Ruby couldn't drag her eyes away from the Irish hunk even though Leo was pulling her up the porch steps. "Wow."

She didn't even realize she'd whispered that thought out loud until Leo stopped and frowned down at her. Smiling up at him weakly, she stepped forward, ready for him to open the front door.

The door opened before she could touch it. In front of her stood the most amazingly attractive woman she'd ever seen. She wasn't much taller or older than Ruby. The woman's hair fell to her waist, a straight, shining curtain of glowing red-gold. Slightly tilted green eyes the color of emeralds peeked out from under the longest, most lush lashes Ruby had ever seen. Her chin was delicately pointed, her nose fine and aristocratic, her lips full and pink. She stared up at Leo, those lips trembling.

Suddenly, Ruby wasn't feeling so good. The woman was looking at Leo with a love so deep Ruby was moved by it. If he had this woman waiting for him to come home, why had he brought Ruby?

"Welcome home, Leo." The woman stepped into his welcoming arms, tears falling down her exquisite face.

"Hi, Mom."

Ruby unclenched her hands, just then realizing she'd been clenching them.

Of course. Mom. Dad's a sex god, and Mom's a cover model. I wonder what Shane and Moira look like? Ruby had never felt quite so frumpy in her life. She was wrinkled from head to toe, her hair a mess, her eyes heavy with fatigue, her makeup long since worn off. Her self confidence took a severe hit. She took a step back, not wanting to intrude on Leo's reunion with his mother.

She didn't get very far. One hard hand fell on her arm, pulling her forward. Leo put his other arm around his mother's shoulders. "Mom, I'd like you to meet Ruby Halloway. Ruby, this is my mother, Aileen Dunne."

"I am pleased to meet you, Ruby. Be welcome in my home." The woman's soft brogue had a hint of Great Britain in it, changing it slightly from the pure Irish purr of her husband's voice.

"Thank you, Mrs. Dunne." Ruby held out her hand in greeting.

Mrs. Dunne promptly took possession of it, pulling Ruby into the house behind her. "Now, call me Aileen, please. And did that son of mine remember to bring everything you need, or did he drag you out of the house so quickly your head spun?"

"Um, number two."

Aileen turned a dark look over her shoulder, and that was when Ruby finally believed that the stunning woman before her really was Leo's mother. No one but a mother could look at a man like that, part exasperation, part love.

"It *was* a bit of an emergency, Mom." Ruby turned to see Leo pushing his hand through his hair, grimacing slightly. "I made sure her cat was taken care of, didn't I?"

Aileen sighed, a sound that only a mother could make, and pulled both of them into her house. Ruby bit her lip on a nervous giggle, knowing laughter wouldn't be welcome at the moment.

Dare to Believe

Leo watched Ruby get her first glimpse of his family home. The cream-colored walls and dark, sturdy wooden furniture wasn't his taste, but his parents adored the old-style look they'd managed to achieve. They'd blended early American with a number of pieces they'd moved from Ireland for a look that was uniquely their own. Framed prints of Ireland mingled with family portraits they'd had taken by mortals. The dark green fabrics of the furniture mingled with the softer, cheerful yellows his mother had strewn about the room in the form of pillows and flowers. The only odd note was an amethyst vase Leo had bought his mother for her birthday two years ago, sitting in pride of place on the mantelpiece. Leo felt a small pang when he saw it. He had to make the effort to get home more often. He hadn't realized how much he missed his family until he saw them.

Ruby, he saw, absorbed it all, her eyes going from object to object while his mother led them into the kitchen.

Moira was busy stirring a pot of stew, her red-gold hair falling in a long braid down her back. Her deep blue eyes, startling in her pale face, shot to his, so full of relief and arrogance he was astonished.

His baby sister had grown up quite a bit while he'd been gone.

He smiled at her, filled with love at the sight of the beautiful woman she'd grown to be over the last few years. "Hi, Moira."

"Leo." She looked him up and down, her eyes full of mischief. "You've certainly filled out. A *lot*."

Leo grimaced. He could feel himself beginning to blush. "Moira, this is Ruby Halloway. Ruby—"

Moira stepped forward with an easy smile, her hands held out. "Moira Dunne, *his*—" she pointed a finger abruptly at Leo,

"—little sister." She shook her head, her lip curled up, amused. "How did Leo wind up with you? You're not at all the bimbo-y type he usually—"

Before she could finish that sentence Leo had her in a headlock, one hand firmly clasped over her lips, his face beet red with, embarrassment. "Ignore everything that comes out of her mouth, okay?" He shot his sister a warning glance. The last thing he needed was for Moira to tell Ruby who, and *what*, they were before he had the chance to.

Ruby raised one eyebrow, aware of the underlying tension in every move the Dunnes were making. If horsing around was how Moira chose to deal with it, Ruby wouldn't step in the way. She noticed that Aileen, far from being upset, had calmly taken her daughter's place at the stove, serenely stirring the stew.

She left brother and sister wrestling amiably and stepped over to Aileen. "Is there anything I can do to help?" She still felt awkward, but the Dunnes were pretty relaxed considering the circumstances. They were treating her like they'd known her for ages. *Almost like one of the family.*

Aileen smiled at her. This close, the faint lines of strain around her eyes were more noticeable. She wondered if there was anything she could do to take some of the burden off the older woman. Sean had come into the kitchen and whispered something in Leo's ear and Leo had nodded in response, his expression pleased. Sean had then moved to his wife, placing a small kiss on the side of her neck before pulling plates from the cupboards.

"That's sweet of you, Ruby, but no." Aileen raised her voice only slightly and the wrestling near the kitchen table came to an abrupt end. "Moira and I have things under control."

"I'll show Ruby to our room, then, Mom. I think we could

both use a shower before we eat." Leo stepped forward, his hair deliciously rumpled, his shirt half out of his pants. Ruby had to tamp down the totally inappropriate spate of lust that gripped her. *For God's sake, girl, get a grip! His mom is standing right there!*

Did he just say our *bedroom?* She looked over at Aileen, wondering how the woman felt about that.

"Dinner in one hour, Leo." His mom didn't even lift her gaze from the stew pot she was stirring.

He took Ruby's hand and began leading her from the room. "We'll be ready."

"Leo?"

"Hmm?"

"Where's your parents' bedroom?"

"Two doors down from ours."

"Oh, hell no."

She pulled against his hand and he stopped with a frown. "What's the problem, kitten?"

"Leo, we can't sleep together with your parents right down the hall!" Her horrified whisper was more of a hiss. He opened the door to their bedroom.

Their bedroom. The shaft of joy and satisfaction that shot through him at that thought would have had him grinning except for one thing. Leo had fully expected an argument from his little kitten when she realized his parents had put them in the same bedroom. He wasn't disappointed, unfortunately. He'd just *known* she was going to be difficult about this. He led her to the upstairs bedroom his father had put their suitcases in. "It's all right, Ruby. If my parents had a problem with it, Dad would have put our suitcases in separate rooms."

Ruby dug her heels in. He had to drag her the rest of the way into their room. He'd have picked her up and thrown her over his shoulder if she'd offered any serious resistance. He'd had a hard enough day without adding a fight with her into the mix.

He began unpacking his suitcase, ignoring the fact that she hadn't moved from where he'd left her. "Unpack, sweetheart, we've got enough time for a quick shower before dinner if you hurry."

She stirred, a frown on her face. She opened her mouth to say something, but bit her lip and looked away instead.

He stopped, a shirt dangling from his fingers. She looked…odd. Like she'd swallowed something sour. "What is it, kitten?"

She shrugged, a small smile chasing away her frown. "Nothing." She began to unpack.

Leo had been around enough women to know that *nothing* usually meant *something*. And *nothing* said in that particular way usually meant *everything*.

He put the shirt down on the bed and went to her, wrapping his arms around her. He inhaled her sweet scent and his cock hardened immediately. "When a woman says nothing the way you just said nothing, I start worrying. Out with it, kitten."

She shrugged again, obviously embarrassed. "It's nothing, really."

"Now you're beginning to terrify me." He bent down and nuzzled her neck through her hair, wallowing in the silky feel of her skin. He felt her shudder when he stroked her earlobe with his tongue and teeth. Suddenly, it had been way too long since he'd been inside her. "C'mon, kitten. Tell me."

"It's stupid."

He licked his way from her earlobe to the top of her shoulder. "Mm-hmm." He'd totally lost track of the conversation, his only goal now to get her out of her clothes and on her knees. Or on the bed. Or anywhere, so long as it involved a lot of naked.

"It's just...you'll think I'm just being whiney."

Danger! Red alert! Red alert!

She jerked in his arms. "Did you just hear a siren?"

He pulled up abruptly, pulling his powers back around him like a cloak. "Um, no, what did it sound like?"

She frowned up at him, confused. "Like the red alert signal from *Star Trek*."

"Oh. Uh, maybe Moira's watching TV."

She relaxed, and he held back a sigh of relief. "Oh. That makes sense. I suppose."

"Now. What's the problem?" No *way* were the words "stupid" or "whiney" going to pass his lips. He had *some* sense of self preservation, after all. He tried to get her to relax by stroking her back soothingly.

"This is *so* juvenile."

Hell. "Spit it out, kitten, you've chewed it enough. What is it?"

She took a deep breath and visibly braced herself. "It's just...well, I mean, your *parents* are down the hall. Aren't they going to, you know, *hear us*?" That last was a furious whisper, her face beet red. She glared up at him.

He stared at her. *How exactly do I want to answer that?*

She rolled her eyes before he could come up with a response. "Never mind. God, I feel like such an idiot for even asking."

"Oh, no, let's get *that* one settled right now." He forcibly walked her over to the bed and sat down, pulling her down onto his knee. He wrapped his arms securely around her waist. "Care to repeat that question?"

She punched him, hard enough to earn a grunt. "Leo! *What if they hear us?*"

"First of all, I'm not twelve years old."

She mumbled something under her breath, but he decided to let it pass.

"Second of all, you're not twelve years old."

She glared up at him through her bangs, looking mutinous.

"Kitten, if it bothered them, Dad would have put us in separate rooms. Do I hear an echo in here? Ow." Leo rubbed the sore spot that was rapidly developing on his chest. *I have got to find a better use for her hands.* "What is the problem here? You came with me, you're here for me, and they put us in the same room because they know you're mine. Do you want to sleep in my sister's room? Because if you do, I'll just sneak in there, and you'll be naked with an audience."

She sighed. "Leo—"

"I need you with me, Ruby." He stared into her eyes, trying desperately to convey with a look what he couldn't yet put into words. It was too soon, too much else was going on, and there were things he still hadn't told her. Things he knew he should tell her, but he wanted to talk to his parents first. "Please."

Again, it was the *please* that won the day for him. That, and the fact that he'd actually argued about keeping her with him. "Okay." She cuddled up against him and he held her, stroking her hair. The part of her that was starting to seriously fall for him was glad she hadn't insisted on moving out of the room despite the oddness of having his parents right down the hall from them. "But I'm still not sure about the whole nookie thing."

"Nookie?" His shoulders quivered under her hands. He sounded like he was trying not to laugh.

Her head tilted to the side and she bit her lip. An idea had occurred to her, brought on by the thought of both getting clean and getting some Leo. She just hoped she was up for it. It had been a really long day and she was starting to wind down, but she was tired of fighting something they both wanted. "Didn't you want to take a shower?" She peeked at him out of the corner of her eye. "We could always take one together. With all that running water, they might not hear anything."

She scraped her nails along the nape of his neck, enjoying the shiver that moved through him. He leaned down, his expression smoldering. She barely suppressed her own shiver when he began nibbling at her ear, taking the lobe between his teeth and doing things that made her wish dinner wasn't in less than an hour.

"Um. Sounds...delicious." His voice was a low growl. His nibbling had migrated to her neck and was lazily heading south. By the time he reached the sensitive juncture of her neck and shoulder she was ready to melt into a puddle of goo. When he reached up and began tweaking her nipple through her shirt she *did* melt into a puddle of goo.

With a low groan he pulled himself away from her long enough to yank her shirt over her head. He bent over her, pulling her in close for a kiss.

"Leo Dunne! If I don't hear water running in five minutes you'll know what's what!"

Ruby looked up at Leo. His eyes were wide and bright with suppressed laughter. "Now you know why I ran away from home." He leaned in and planted a swift kiss on her smiling lips. "Yes, Ma," he yelled, loud enough to make Ruby wince.

"Should I make sure you wash behind your ears?" Ruby giggled. She hadn't felt like this since she was a teenager.

"And other places?" His puppy-dog hopeful expression had her hiding her face in his shirt, overcome with the giggles.

He picked her up easily and carried her into the shower. "Let's conserve water, shall we?"

"Mmm-hmm."

Leo slipped quietly out of the room. She'd been too tired to make love before nodding off. His kitten was totally exhausted. She'd slipped on a tiny, silky little cream colored thing that she swore was a nightgown and he swore was a wet dream come true. She'd crawled into bed and passed out soon after dinner, curled up around him like the kitten he'd named her. The shower gymnastics he would have loved to indulge in had been interrupted by his pest of a sister, banging on the door and yelling for all she was worth that dinner was ready and he'd better get his Fae butt down the stairs before his mother came up for him. Perhaps it was just as well. He doubted she would have lasted long enough to eat if they'd made love.

He'd just have to make sure he took better care of her from now on. He didn't like it when his little kitten was all tuckered out for the wrong reasons.

He hadn't understood why Ruby had glared at his sister when they'd finally headed down, until he'd heard her mutter under her breath that his butt was fine, thank you very much. He'd nearly burst out laughing.

Dinner had been a unique mixture of tension and curiosity. No mention was made of Shane or his kidnapping at the table. Instead everyone had focused on Ruby. They'd done their best to make her feel welcome, but there'd been no denying the gentle inquisition his parents had put her through. But his kitten was tough. She'd answered each question with dignity and a light touch of humor that had won over both of his parents. He hadn't needed to see his father's nod of approval or his mother's smile to know they'd both liked her tremendously.

Moira, however, seemed to be reserving judgment. Oh, she liked Ruby, and made that plain. Yet in that odd sisterly sort of way she'd managed to convey that she wasn't certain that Ruby was good enough for him. He wondered if he'd be as big a pain in the ass when she brought *her* mate home to meet them one day, and shuddered. The thought of his baby sister letting a man touch her made him want to punch something.

His family was waiting for him in the kitchen, Mom making a pot of coffee, Dad chatting quietly with Moira. They all looked at him when he entered, and suddenly he knew how Dad, and to some extent Shane, felt during these family meetings. Each of them was staring at him like he could somehow make everything right. He took his seat, accepting the coffee his mother handed him with a small smile.

"Is Ruby settled in then?"

The lyrical notes of his mother's tongue flowed over him, soothing something in his spirit he hadn't even realized had been abraded. "Aye, Mum. She's sleeping peacefully." The language, so long unused, came to him easily, surprising him.

"You're sure she's the one, then?" Moira's question, though not unexpected, still grated.

"Aye, I'm sure. Everything about her calls to my senses in a way no other woman ever has."

The confidence in his voice had Moira sitting back, nodding thoughtfully. "Does she know of us?"

"You mean does she know that when we aren't glamoured we sprout pointy ears and speak in Sidhe? No, I haven't told her that yet, considering I just finally got her into my bed last night."

Moira unconsciously fingered the delicately tapered point of one ear. "When do you plan on telling her? Before or after the ceremony?"

"Moira. Enough." Sean's voice was stern. "Ruby's human. Leo will need to lead her up to it."

"Rent *Lord of the Rings* first, it might help." Moira grinned at him, that cheeky one that never failed to worry him. She leaned forward. "Ask her if she thinks Legolas is hot."

"I can't wait to see who you mate, Moira. I hope he's human." Leo bopped her on the head with an oven mitt, making her giggle. "Maybe he'll think Legolas is hot."

She bared her teeth at him in a smiling snarl. Aileen took the oven mitt from her before Moira could bop him back. "Enough. Leo, let us know if you need help explaining things to her."

Meaning, explain them soon, before you head back to D.C.

"Yes, Mum."

Sean stood, and all eyes turned to him. Leo's dad was one of the most easygoing men he knew, until one of his own was threatened. Leo had sensed the tremendous anger Sean was hiding the moment he'd stepped foot on his father's land.

It was never, ever wise to piss off an earth sprite.

"I've got feelers out to all of my cousins in this country and Ireland, just to be safe," Sean said. He'd planted his feet wide, his thumbs hooked into the loops on his jeans, his face stern. He looked like a warrior readying his troops for battle. "The earth spirits allied with us will keep me apprised of what's going on. If he's anywhere near one of them, they'll let me know."

"I've contacted some of the Sidhe who still speak with me,

Dare to Believe

and they've assured me they've heard no mention of Shane." Aileen's face was calm and composed. Her hands were white-knuckled around her mug. She took a deep breath, her jaw determined, her eyes hard, and Leo was suddenly, inexplicably afraid. "There's someone who owes me a favor—"

"No, Aileen."

The iron in his father's voice surprised him. "Who?" His parents shared a long, unreadable look. "Who owes you a favor, Mum? If they can find Shane, we should call them."

"That favor may come at a price we're not prepared to pay, Leo."

Leo turned to his father, but Sean's stern gaze never left Aileen.

"*He* owes *me*, Sean."

"And he'll turn that to his advantage."

"He can find my baby, Sean Patrick! Let him find my baby!"

Aileen finally broke, tears running silently down her face. Sean's eyes closed at the sight of his mate's fear and pain. The helplessness he obviously felt in the face of her grief was something Leo hoped he'd never suffer through with Ruby. Bad enough his brother was missing. If it was his child, the child of his beloved mate? He didn't know if he'd be in any better shape than his mother was in.

Leo huffed out a breath and exchanged his own glance with Moira. Who the hell was his mother talking about?

"You've called him?" Sean's voice was weary.

"Aye."

Sean nodded at his wife's whispered response. "So be it, then."

"Who are you two talking about?"

The sudden gust of wind heralded the advent of a tornado

of power in the middle of the Dunne kitchen. Out of that tornado stepped a tall, slender man with waist length red hair and laughing blue eyes in a face that would have made Michelangelo weep. The tornado was dressed in a dark blue poet's shirt that matched his eyes and tight leather pants that showcased a slim build. Knee-high leather boots completed the look.

Every hair on Leo's body stood on end at the sight of that slender young man.

"Robin Goodfellow, for my sins," the figure said, bowing extravagantly. He looked up from his bow, cocked his head at Sean, and laughed out loud.

"Shit. *Shit.* Robin-fucking-Goodfellow owes Mom a *favor?*" Leo paced back and forth in the front yard, wiping at his face wearily.

"Ah, but I'm not fucking at the moment, dear fellow, although I might wish I was."

Leo swung around and gulped. Robin Goodfellow was sitting on the hood of his Navigator, legs crossed Indian style, a leer on those boyish features. "You see, when I received that call from your absolutely ravishing mother, I was hip deep in a pool with a pair of Naiad twins. Alas and alack, I doubt the lovely ladies waited for my return." With an exaggerated sigh, Robin brushed his long red hair back with an effeminate sweep of his hand. Leo noticed that the Hob's nails were painted black. "Now, if *I* had a prime piece waiting in my bed for me the way you do, I doubt I'd be out here worrying about someone like me."

"Stay away from Ruby." Leo didn't even recognize the growl that erupted from his throat.

Those brilliant blue eyes flashed completely green before

auburn lashes drifted down, hiding them. The leer turned into a smug smile. "Bonded, boy?"

"Not yet," Leo forced out between clenched teeth. He'd never been more terrified in his life. He was insane. He'd practically challenged the Hob!

Bright blue eyes lifted up and studied him, all humor, all pretenses gone, and Leo realized he was seeing the true Hob, Oberon's Blade, for the first time.

"Well, isn't that a shame, seeing as you're the reason Shane's missing."

"Damn. The marriage contract?"

The Hob nodded. "The marriage contract."

Leo began swearing, a blend of Fae and English. "I thought that old contract was null and void, due to Mom bonding Dad. Why are they trying to enforce it now?"

"Power, Leo. Why else would a family like the Malmaynes do this?"

Leo stared at Robin, trying desperately to see past the unholy amusement in his deep blue eyes. "You're certain the Malmaynes have him?"

"Yes. When you turned down the match with the eldest daughter, they began plotting how to get you to change your mind. From what I was able to gather, their original target was Moira." Leo's hands clenched into fists. "When they couldn't get to her, Shane was their next best target. You were too closely guarded, too into the human world for them to touch directly." Leo turned away from the red-haired devil sitting on his SUV and stared up at his window. "The plan was to force your hand. Your Ruby will complicate things."

"These contracts are usually considered null and void in the advent of a truebond."

Robin's expression turned icy. "When power is involved, sometimes these things can get…tricky. And since it was Aileen's family that wrote up the original contract…" The Hob shrugged. Leo paced, aware of the Hob's eyes following him.

"Is Kaitlynn involved?"

"The Malmayne girl would rather have you willing than not."

"That's not what I asked."

The devil grinned at him. "No. It's not."

Leo listened to the crickets and tried to unclench his hands. "Will they go after Ruby?"

One red brow lifted in thought. "Possibly. Until you complete the bonding the two of you are vulnerable. Sidhe like the Malmaynes won't care that your bond is a True one, only that she stands in the way of their ambitions." Robin shrugged. "No offence, but if your mother had followed through on her own contract instead of falling for the leprechaun none of this would have happened."

"And Shane, Moira and I wouldn't exist, and Mom would have been miserable."

"So fighting for love is worth it, then?"

Leo glared at Robin. "If my mother feels for my father half of what I feel for Ruby, then yes. It's more than worth it."

That disconcerting flash of green appeared in Robin's eyes again, and for a moment Leo was frozen in place. For one blinding second he knew exactly how the Hob felt.

Unbearable, unutterable, unending, envious. *Alone.*

Then those eyes were shuttered once again by a fall of auburn lashes and Leo was freed. "Then fight." A gust of wind blew by, blurring the edges of the Hob, blowing him away like a sand sculpture. "When the Malmaynes arrive, fight."

Chapter Five

"Any word on your brother?"

Ruby, half asleep, whispered those words as he crawled into bed. Leo winced. He'd hoped not to wake her. His kitten had been exhausted and needed her sleep. "Yeah. I'll tell you about it in the morning."

"It is morning." She sounded more alert, damn it. He was *so* tired. "Do they know yet who has your brother?"

Leo took a deep breath, the events of the night before once again pushing to the forefront of his mind. He could feel his muscles tensing and tried his best to get himself to relax. "Yeah. We know who has him."

She sat up abruptly, holding the sheet demurely over her breasts. "That's wonderful! Do the police know? Is he okay? Is he on his way home?"

Leo pulled on her arm, yawning so hard it felt like his jaw would crack. "Down, kitten. It's not that easy."

She resisted the pull of his arm and frowned down at him. "What isn't that easy?"

Leo sighed, and wondered how to explain to her the intricacies of the Seelie court system. "Shane was kidnapped by a...rival family."

She stared at him, her eyes blank with incomprehension.

"Huh?"

He sighed, rubbing his face tiredly. "Can I get some sleep first, please? I promise I'll explain everything to you after we've eaten breakfast." He allowed his weariness to show through the glamour he normally kept up, gratified when she frowned and traced the dark circles under his eyes. "Please?"

Her frown deepened. "You're hiding something from me, aren't you?"

The fact that she could already read him so easily was both encouraging and disturbing. "I promise I'll explain everything, even the stuff I'm not sure you'll understand, or believe. But I'd really like some sleep first, okay?"

She huffed. "Well. Okay. But he's okay, right? I mean, your family has at least that much assurance?"

"Yes, Shane is okay."

She nodded, obviously reluctant to drop the subject. His curious kitten. He watched her slip back under the covers, the ridiculous slip of cream-colored silk sliding along her body. He held out his arms. When she turned trustingly to spoon him, he sighed in relief, burying his face in the fragrance of her hair.

He was asleep with minutes, his overworked mind and body finally taking their toll on him.

Ruby woke up alone, but she hadn't forgotten the talk they'd had in the middle of the night. She got up and dressed quickly. She started down the stairs, eager to hear Leo's news.

She could hear the sounds of the Dunne family talking, their voices rising and falling in that weird Gaelic-sounding language. Ruby entered the kitchen to Aileen's voice rising above the rest, full of outrage and authority.

"Moira Eileen Dunne!" Aileen's voice stopped her daughter

Dare to Believe

in her tracks. Moira had decked Leo, punched him straight in the nose and landed him flat on his ass. The beautiful girl had been going after her brother for round two.

He was stumbling to his feet when Moira growled, the sound barely human. "Shane's gone, and it's all your fault!"

Leo flinched, his face stricken. He turned abruptly on his heel and walked out of the kitchen.

Aileen sighed and rubbed her forehead.

"Leo?" Moira made a move to go out the door, her expression just as stricken as her brother's. Her mother grabbed her arm and began quietly talking to her, chastising her.

Ruby ignored the other two women and followed Leo. She found him on the front porch, clutching at the railing with white knuckled fingers and staring up at the sky with haunted eyes. She didn't know what to do or say. She didn't know anything about his family or the way it worked. So she did the only thing she could think of. She walked up behind him, wrapped her arms around his waist, and held on for dear life.

He was tense in her arms for the first few moments, almost rejecting the comfort of her touch. Finally he turned and gathered her close, his face buried in her hair, his arms wrapped around her so tightly it hurt. She wanted to kill Moira. She'd never wanted to kill someone before, but if she had Moira Dunne alone in that moment, Leo would be minus a sister. She held him, stroked his hair, and resolved that she would get to the bottom of whatever had caused Moira to hurt the man in her arms so badly that he shook with it.

When Moira stepped out on the porch, looking both sheepish and penitent, Ruby couldn't find it in her to forgive her. Yet.

Ruby shook her head slightly, trying to get the other

79

woman to go away. She didn't think Leo would want his sister seeing him so vulnerable. With a slight nod, the girl went back inside, and Ruby went back to trying to soothe the slowly calming man.

Jaden stared through the one-way glass at the unique man on the other side. Shane Joloun Dunne lay sprawled on his back, his dark blue eyes glued to the ceiling, a look of total concentration on his face. He was completely naked, not that Jaden was looking.

Okay, yes, he was. The man had a hell of a physique.

"Why the hell is he naked?" Jaden asked, turning to Malmayne the elder. *Other than for my viewing pleasure, that is.*

Cullen Malmayne looked at him blankly. "In case he tries to escape, of course."

Jaden nodded, and then shook his head. "What kind of spy movies have you been watching?"

Cullen's snort of aggravation was music to Jaden's ears. "Shane will be too embarrassed to run through the streets of, may the gods help us, Omaha, completely nude."

Jaden blinked, his dark eyes glittering with amusement. If it were *him* behind that glass wall, you bet your ass he'd be running around Omaha stark naked if he had to. But from what he'd seen, when the time came Shane wouldn't have that problem.

"Any clue as to what he's doing?" Cullen's voice was mildly curious, like a man wondering what his dog was doing and why.

Making himself clothes, Jaden thought. He was pretty sure the hybrid had some secreted around his cell, not that Jaden would tell. Jaden shook his head, turning once again to stare at

Shane and hoping like hell the man would be ready soon. Jaden hated working for Malmayne the Elder and the Deranged Darling.

"Any word from the Dunne's?" Jaden waited for the answer he knew would be coming.

"No."

He nodded, not really surprised, when the door behind them opened.

"Has Leo called?"

Jaden shuddered at the saccharin sound of Kaitlynn's voice, his eyes never leaving the two-way glass. *Much better view, anyway.*

"No, my dear, he hasn't. He should contact us soon, however." Jaden kept watch on Cullen and Kaitlynn out of the corner of his eye. Cullen moved towards his daughter, his voice soothing and mild. *Crazy bitch,* he thought, watching a slight movement of Shane's hand. A shimmer of dark blue silk appeared in his hand and was swiftly thrust under the mattress. The hybrid's eyes shut wearily, his task complete. For the moment.

Jaden grinned, careful to hide his teeth. It was only a matter of time before both his and the hybrid's plans could be set in motion.

"You want to tell me what that was all about?"

The quiet question didn't surprise him. The calm acceptance did. He figured she deserved some answers, starting with who, and what, he was, and why he needed her with him.

They were sitting in the barn, in the hayloft, staring up at the sky. He hadn't wanted to go back into the house just yet, hadn't wanted to face Moira's accusations or his mother's understanding. So he'd taken his kitten to the barn and up into the hayloft, his favorite spot, and settled her down on the hay.

He felt her patient gaze on him, but had no idea how to explain to her everything that was going on without revealing the family's secrets. He didn't know if she was ready for that. Unfortunately, he didn't think he had a choice in the matter.

"Just spit it out, Leo."

That faint hint of impatience pulled a reluctant grin from him. He settled back with a sigh, his eyes fixed on the sky out the barn doors. It was a beautiful day, the sky bright and blue, with what few clouds there were only adding to the overall picture. The Dunne lands were extremely fertile; his father's magic saw to that. He could see him in the distance, working his lands, talking to some of the other people who helped to run the huge amount of acreage Sean owned.

Leo didn't often brag about his father, but the man had just as much talent for making money as he did for growing corn and potatoes. His parents chose to live in the house they did rather than something more elaborate, keeping a low profile and enjoying the benefit of having their neighbors feel free with them.

"Leo. You're stalling."

He sighed. "I'm not stalling, kitten. I'm trying to figure out how to explain the unexplainable."

He looked down into her face and felt his heart roll over. The patient sympathy in there, the warmth and trust he could see, nearly unmanned him. He resolved then and there to answer any question truthfully, even if it drove her from him.

Not that he would let her get very far. "Where do you want me to start?"

"Why haven't you called the police?"

Leo nodded, his eyes once more on the horizon. He didn't even see it, being too busy trying to gather his thoughts. *Time to come clean.* "Two reasons. One, because there's not a damn thing the police could do to help us, and two, it's forbidden to involve them in affairs such as this."

She stared up at him, puzzled. "I...don't understand."

She dropped her gaze down to their joined hands, feeling his tremble slightly in hers, and knew he was working up his courage to tell her something he was pretty sure she didn't want to hear. "Leo?" She could hear the uncertainty in her own voice and winced. "What's going on?" A horrible thought struck her, and she blurted it out without thinking. "Shane *was* kidnapped, right?"

Leo grimaced, his expression rueful. He looked down at her, and something about his expression told her that this was about more than just his brother's kidnapping. "Yes, Shane was kidnapped, and Moira's right. It's my fault. Partly."

"Why, because of your money? Did they think you'd pay a huge ransom or something?"

Leo huffed out a laugh. "I wish. It would be a lot less complicated if it were that simple."

"Tell me why, Leo."

The forced way he blew out his breath let her know it would be bad. *Very* bad. "It has to do with a marriage contract."

"A what?" Confused, Ruby stared up at him.

"A marriage contract. An arranged marriage was set up by my mother's father, Armand Joloun, and a man named Cullen Malmayne. Both sides thought to benefit from a marriage of power between Cullen's son and my mother, but my grandfather is the one who approached the Malmaynes. Which is part of why this whole thing is so screwed up."

"Your grandfather's name sounds French, but your mom is Irish. Isn't she?"

"Half Irish. Moira's named for our grandmother, and Mom was raised in Ireland with her."

Ruby thought about that, absorbing it, and let it go. It had no real relevance. "Okay, so your grandfather and this Malmayne dude wrote out a contract, swearing to wed their children to each other. I gather Aileen wasn't so thrilled with the idea?"

"Oh, at first she had no real objection. It isn't all that unusual, and from what I understand Duncan Malmayne is a fairly attractive man, wealthy and powerful. But Mom met Dad, and that was pretty much the end of that."

"So, what, the Malmaynes sued for breach of contract?"

Leo sighed. "Here's where it gets tricky. Mom and Dad share a unique bond, something that should have nullified the contract, but apparently there was an escape clause written in by my grandfather. In the event that either Duncan or my mother was unable to fulfill the terms, it would devolve to the next generation of both families. In other words, any one of their children could make an arranged marriage."

"And they want Shane to fulfill this clause in the contract?"

Leo looked at her, and Ruby felt her heart sink. "No. They want me."

They can't have you! Ruby shivered with the force of that denial. "Why you?"

Leo opened his mouth, but nothing came out at first. "I'm not quite certain how to explain this." He rubbed his hand over the back of his neck nervously. The other hand picked up hers and clasped it warmly, his thumb moving in soothing strokes over the back of her fingers.

"Open mouth, spit out words. C'mon, Leo, it can't be *that* bad."

"There's something you need to know first." His eyes were glued to their joined hands.

"Okay, what?"

"I will never, ever, do anything to harm you. You mean more to me than you could possibly understand yet. And if I have my way you and the Malmaynes will never cross paths." He clasped both of her hands in between his, his expression more serious than any she'd seen on his face yet. She could practically feel him willing her to believe in him. "Do you understand what I'm saying?"

She shook her head. She was starting to get scared. "Leo, *what is going on?*"

He took a deep breath, and her world exploded in light. She was forced to close her eyes against the blinding brilliance. When she opened them again, she was shocked speechless.

The hay bales and farming equipment had disappeared. Instead she found herself inside a huge sapphire tent, the edges and "windows" detailed in delicate gold Arabic scrollwork. The floor was completely covered in brightly colored silk pillows of every hue imaginable. A small gold table had been set up against one wall. On it sat a carafe of wine and a plate of candied dates. Fragrant oil lamps hung from the three poles holding the tent up, sending the delicious scent of vanilla into the air.

Wide-eyed she turned to look at what was behind her. It was only then that she realized that she could feel the soft caress of silk against her bare flesh. She looked down.

"Holy crap!" The scanty harem costume, consisting of two barely-there red scarves over her breasts and long, sheer red skirt held at her waist by a gold belt, left absolutely nothing to the imagination.

"Hmmm, I do like you in red, kitten."

She stared, her eyes wide as saucers, towards the front of the tent.

There, in all his half-naked, white-garbed splendor, was Leo. His white pants were gathered at the ankles and waist with gold ties and his chest and feet were bare. Golden armbands encircled both of his biceps. His expression held a glimmer of amusement mixed with a healthy dose of lust.

He entered the tent, moving with the grace of a panther. Any other man of Ruby's acquaintance would have slipped and fallen on the silk pillows. Leo glided over them, his feet barely making an impression. Her nipples tightened in anticipation at his predatory expression. His gaze roved over her body with unmistakable possession.

Ruby gulped and bit her lip. "Leo?"

"Don't be afraid, kitten. Remember, I'll never, ever hurt you."

"What's going on?"

"Trust me."

"Toto, I've got a feeling we're not in Nebraska anymore," Ruby whispered.

Leo stopped. His lips twitched. "You're about to be ravished by a Seelie Sidhe lord and you're misquoting *The Wizard of Oz* at me? I think I may be insulted."

Ruby blinked, her rampant sense of humor once again threatening to get her into trouble. "First off, a Sealy is a mattress—"

"You're welcome to lie on me anytime."

"Second, you are *so* not a she."

Dare to Believe

"Shtheee. It's pronounced *Shthee*."

"Uh-huh. Lord? That I believe. Hell, you're the absolute King of Bullshit."

Leo sighed and pinched the bridge of his nose. "Somehow, this isn't going quite the way I expected."

Ruby could practically feel the light bulb settling over her head. She sat up carefully. "Seelie Sidhe lord."

Leo eyed her warily and nodded.

"You're an *elf*?"

Leo frowned. "Sidhe."

"Like Legolas?"

"Ruby!"

"Oh! Galadriel! Can you do the glowy pond thing, too?"

Leo flopped down on the pillows next to her, his breath huffing out in an exasperated laugh. "No, Frodo, I can't."

"Hey!" She sniffed. "I at least get to be Arwen. Hell, I'll take Éowyn." She waved a hand regally. "You can be Gimli."

She dissolved into helpless giggles. Leo rolled over and pulled her under him, one dark brow rising arrogantly. "Ruby, I really am a Seelie Sidhe lord."

She was laughing too hard to answer. He sighed, and pushed his hair back over his ears, allowing their delicately tapered points to show. "Ruby, I have no glamour on me now. Look at me. *Really* look at me."

He had to wait until her giggles died down, and that took a bit of time. They had a slightly hysterical twinge to them that even she could hear. Once they did, she really took a good, hard look at him.

The differences were subtle. His ears were slightly tapered into delicate points. His eyes had an otherworldly glow to them that made them gleam brightly in the lamplight. His skin glittered with sparkles of gold, the effect when he moved erotic. The most exotic change, however, were his pupils. Human pupils were round. His pupils were oval. Not much of a change, and easily disguised, but obviously not human.

Ruby caressed his ear with a wondering hand. Her fingertips gently brushed over the tapered points. He shuddered, his eyes closing in exquisite pain.

"Do you know how long it's been since someone's done that for me?"

She smirked, feeling incredibly sexy all of a sudden. "Erogenous zone?"

"Oh, very much so." He opened his eyes, a sensuous smile curving his lips. He stared down at her barely covered breasts, the sensuous smile heating. "How do you like my fantasy?" She raised one cynical brow, loving it when he chuckled. "At least you're wearing clothes. I'd have preferred you naked."

"I almost am!"

"Yes. Operative word: *almost*."

"Pig."

"That's *Lord* Pig, thank you very much."

"How are you doing this?" Ruby rested her hand on his shoulder, brushing at it to see if the gold sparkles came off in her hand. They didn't.

"It's called glamour. What you see around you isn't actually here. It's…all in our heads. A shared fantasy, if you will."

"An illusion?"

"Not quite. If someone were to take a picture of us right now, it would show the two of us still in the hayloft. To you, however, everything feels real. I could take you outside, place you on my stallion and ride off into the desert with you, and to you it would all seem incredibly real."

"And this is your fantasy? To be sheik to my houri?"

He brushed his thumb across one of her taught nipples. "Can you blame me?"

She stared up at him, that wicked sense of humor starting up again. "Man, you must have had some incredible jack-off material when you were a teenager."

He blinked, stilling above her. "What?" He sounded like he was choking on something. More than likely it was his own laughter.

"Picture this," she waved her hand around, encompassing the tent, "but with a naked Playboy bunny in my place."

"Um, it doesn't quite work like that, and I'd rather picture you naked."

"Oh? How does it work?"

"I can't really craft a fantasy and project it into my own mind. For me, it would be a daydream, just like anyone else's." He smiled, the expression crossing his face slow and wicked. His thumb caressed her bottom lip. The butterfly touch left her wanting more. "I *can* craft a fantasy of my own making and project it into *our* senses. Sight, taste, touch, all of them would respond to the magic as if everything were really there. Or..."

Ruby wasn't certain she liked the speculative gleam in his eye. "What?"

"Or..."

The lights began to swirl together in a kaleidoscope of color, whirling sickeningly around them as the tent, and everything in it, disappeared. She closed her eyes against the sudden onslaught of her senses as everything, sight, smell, even taste became hypersensitive.

When the maelstrom of sensation died down, Ruby opened

her eyes. She blinked and gasped. She was staring at her deepest, darkest sexual fantasy, the one she wouldn't admit even on her deathbed. "What in the world?"

She stood at the street corner near the old deli where she'd grown up. Traffic was non-existent. It often was late on a Sunday night. The chalkboard sign just outside Dooley's Bar and Grill proclaimed it Suds n' Spuds Sunday. Ruby felt herself relax, the fantasy taking over her body and mind. She stood under the glare of the streetlamp, totally secure, totally safe, knowing that *he* would be riding up any minute now to pick her up and take her away.

She wore tight leather pants, so tight you could almost see the cleft of her pussy. Her black leather halter top left her midriff bare and made the most of her cleavage. Her navel was pierced with an electric blue stone. On her feet were high-heeled leather boots. She was dressed to kick ass. She knew, if she took her clothes off, there'd be no underwear to get in the way of whatever *he* wanted to do to her.

Her hair was pulled up in a cascading fall that drifted over one shoulder. At her throat was a diamond collar. Something about the collar felt strange, different from her usual fantasy, but she didn't move from under the streetlamp to check it in the window of the deli. If she did she'd lose the safety and security the light provided. She knew, without having to look in a mirror, that her makeup was smoky, her lips blood red. Her nails were painted the same crimson color, and if she took off one of the ridiculous high heels her toenails would be the same.

She looked over her shoulder and blinked.

Behind her stood every single man she'd ever felt slighted by, including Bobby Pencil-Dick. Each and every one of them stared at her with a yearning expression.

But she didn't belong to them. She belonged only to *him*.

Dare to Believe

A strange rumbling sound pierced the darkness of the night. She turned back and looked down the road. She could see the bright headlight break through the damp fog and felt butterflies begin to dance in her stomach. The sensation was so intense she pressed her hands to her middle. The motorcycle came purring up to a complete stop at the curb right in front of her.

The man on the cycle was to die for. Rich leather covered a lean, muscular figure that had her mouth watering in reaction. He swung his leg off the bike, pulling the leather taught over the firm globes of his ass. He reached up and pulled off the helmet and set it on the seat. He seemed to flow into the light. He stopped before her, leaned down and gave her a swift, hard kiss that rocked her back on her heels.

When Leo pulled back, his gaze went straight for the diamond collar at her throat. With a smile of satisfaction and possession, he took her hand and started to lead her to the cycle.

"Don't even think I'll share you with any of the figments, kitten. You're all mine."

She blinked and shook off some of the effects of the glamour he'd woven around her. That part of the fantasy hadn't even crossed her mind. Picking and choosing between the panting suitors at her back, leaving them all in her high-heeled dust as she rode off into the night with her fantasy lover, no longer had any appeal.

It seemed Leo wasn't taking any chances, however. Apparently he'd decided to skip straight to the riding off portion of tonight's entertainment.

With the bold recklessness this particular fantasy tended to inspire in her, she asked, "How do you know I'm ready to leave them behind and have only you?" Of course, she *was* ready to ride off, but who said she couldn't play a little too?

Leo stopped and turned. He hooked one finger in the diamond collar and pulled her towards him in a move that screamed possession. "You're mine, kitten. You wear my collar. Or didn't you notice?"

Her fingers flew to her collar, tracing over the design on the front. Unhooking the clasp, she removed the collar and turned it to look at it.

It *was* different from the collar she usually pictured. Four strands of diamonds still made up the collar. The difference? In the center of the collar, in ruby chips circled in emeralds, were the letters *LD*. He'd collared her with his initials.

Gently taking the collar from her hands, Leo moved to fasten it around her throat. One black brow rose in challenge when she started to move back a step. "I wouldn't do that, kitten." He moved closer to her, crowding her smaller frame with his, surrounding her with his strength and warmth, subtly threatening her with his blatant sexuality. "You know you're meant to ride off with me. You belong to me."

When he reached out to clasp the collar around her throat once again she stood still, watching his hands. A flash of gold caught her attention. When he lowered his hands, she grasped the left one, turning it so that she could see the ring that gleamed there on his finger.

The gold ring was on his ring finger, right where a wedding ring would rest. The black onyx was slightly oval, like Leo's pupils. Engraved in the face of the onyx were the initials *RH*. Without words, he'd told her that he belonged to her just as much as she belonged to him. Wondering, she looked down at the ring, touched beyond belief. In a gesture that was pure instinct, she pulled his hand to her lips and kissed the ring.

His eyes flared brightly, their green glow intensifying. If she hadn't known before that he wasn't human she'd certainly have known it now. He'd lost control over his personal glamour. She could see the points of his elfin ears through the strands of his hair. The gold dusting of his skin glimmered under the lamplight. With a rough, inarticulate sound he bent down to capture her lips in a searing kiss that claimed her as thoroughly as his body had two nights ago.

She felt one of his hands tangle in her hair and roughly clasp the back of her head. His other hand moved to her hip. She felt herself being herded backwards out of the lamplight, into the shadows, and she struggled briefly.

"It's safe, kitten. I'm here. Nothing can hurt you."

She felt herself relax at his roughly whispered words, up until she felt the bricks of the building against her bare back. Leo bit into the side of her neck, his mouth working, sucking at her neck, marking her as his for all the world to see. He undid the fastening of her halter top, pulling the strands down, exposing her breasts to the cool night air.

She looked with dazed eyes over his shoulder at the figments of her imagination, those few men whose attention she'd so desperately craved at one time or another, and let them go with no regrets. For her, now, there was only Leo. The figments watching them didn't matter, only Leo's hands did. He began to greedily pull and tweak her nipples into diamond-hard points, palming the weight of her breasts, commanding her body's responses.

Gasping for breath, Ruby decided two could play at that game. She reached down with one hand and began to rub his erection through his pants. She pulled the zipper down in a frenzy when he dipped his head down, sucking on her nipple as if he were a starving man and she a five-course meal.

"God, Leo, don't stop." She was panting with desperation,

eager to feel his silken heat in her hands. She pulled his erection out of his pants and stroked it up and down as he suckled her.

"If you don't stop that this will be over before it's started," he growled. He shifted to her other breast and took the nipple between his teeth. He nibbled it, smiling against her when she gasped in pleasure. In response she moved her hand faster on his throbbing cock. He yanked at her zipper, pulling frantically at her pants. "God, kitten, you're killing me."

"Good." Ruby wiggled slightly as he pulled her pants down, sighing her pleasure when he stroked and petted her soaking wet pussy. He pinched her clit almost roughly, smothering her scream with a kiss that practically devoured her.

With a quiet oath Leo tore his mouth from her. He took her hand off his cock, tugging and pushing till he had her positioned facing the wall, both hands spread, her ass cocked back and waiting for him. "Does it excite you to know the figments are watching us, kitten?" He stroked her ass, holding her in place within the cage of his body. He leaned against her, brushing his erection between the cleft of her buttocks in a hypnotic rhythm.

"What? Who? God, Leo, could you fuck me already? I'm dying here!"

Leo laughed under his breath at the rough tone of her voice. In one swift move he sheathed himself in the tight, wet heat of her body, stealing her gasp of pleasure with another rough kiss. She felt tighter this way, unable to spread her legs because of her pants down around her knees. Her pussy clung to his cock, holding him to her, reluctant to let him go.

Leo ended the kiss and looked down as he thrust his shaft in and out of her body, watching the gleaming length sink in, each move causing the woman under him to moan and gasp in delight. When she tried to wiggle her ass in an attempt to get him deeper he slapped it, causing the globe to ripple enticingly.

Her gasp at the sting of his palm turned to a moan as he gave her what she wanted, moving deeper into her as he pushed her hard up against the wall. One hand held on to her hip and pulled her to him, back and forth, forcing him in even further. The other hand dipped down between her thighs and began strumming her clit between his two fingers.

"Oh, oh God, Leo, that feels so good."

"Yeah, it does. Can you come for me, baby?"

She did with a muffled shriek even before he was done asking. She bit her lip to keep from screaming, something Leo didn't like. He wanted to hear her scream, but it was too late. Leo felt the climax rip through her and, with a surprised cry, felt himself come deep inside her. He pounded into her as the last rippling echoes of her climax set off his own.

Leo shuddered against her. Golden sparkles drifted around them and settled on her skin like fairy lights. Inside and out, he surrounded her, filled her senses until nothing else existed but him. He collapsed against her, pushing her almost roughly into the bricks, both of them gasping for air. She rested her cheek against the brick, her face turned towards his. A satisfied smile drifted across her face.

His breath tickled her ear as he whispered against her, "Mine."

With a sigh, she closed her eyes. "Yours." He felt his breath hitch before he buried his face in her neck with a contented sigh.

Chapter Six

When Ruby opened her eyes, they were back in the hayloft. She was on her stomach, her pants down around her knees. Leo lay over her like a dead man, panting lightly, his nose still buried in the side of her neck as if breathing in her scent. With a huffed little laugh, she whispered, "I gather not everything just now was an illusion?"

"Nope," he breathed against her neck.

She shivered at the intimate sensation. "All I can say is, that was one hell of a mind fuck."

"Gives a whole new meaning to the word, doesn't it?" The rich satisfaction in his voice made her grin. She could feel his lazy smile against the side of her neck. One of his hands reached up and tangled their fingers together as he slid off to the side. He cradled her in his arms and she settled against him, content to be held.

The lay together like that for a while, getting their breath back and enjoying the feel of each other, until thoughts and feelings began to race through her head again. "Leo?"

"Yeah?"

"How old are you?"

He sighed, pulling his softened cock out of her body and rolling onto his back. "Are you sure you want the answer to that?"

She looked over at him, his glamour down, that gold-dusted skin even more exotic in the mundane hayloft they were in now. "Yeah, I want to know."

"I'm ninety-three years old."

She blinked. "Wow. You look good for your age." When he sighed wearily she pressed a soft kiss to his cheek, trying to reassure him. "I know. Elves are immortal, right? Unless someone kills them?"

"Try long-lived rather than immortal and you'd be closer."

All of the impossibilities of a relationship with Leo began to rear their ugly heads. "That means when I'm old and wrinkly—"

"You won't be."

The note of complete certainty in his voice confused her. "Uh, give me about forty years and I will be."

He shook his head. "That's the other thing I need to explain to you." He sat up and began pulling up his pants. "You've heard the stories of a man riding off with a Sidhe lass to Underhill, only to return three hundred years later and age all of those years in one day?"

"Um, yeah. I think a lot of people have heard that story."

He zipped up his pants, and then looked at her. "It's true." He shrugged at her complete shock. "Okay, the part about Underhill isn't true. The not aging part was."

"And the aging-three-hundred-years-in-a-day part?"

He took a deep breath. "Also true."

"Leo…"

He couldn't help but respond to the sudden fear in her voice. He held up one hand. "Please, let me explain." With infinite care, he pulled her jeans back over her hips, batting her hands away when she went to do up her zipper. It was his right, his privilege to care for his mate. "When a Sidhe finds his mate, he binds her to him. There are three steps to the bonding, the first being the Claiming."

"What's the Claiming?"

He looked up at her, then back down at the ground. "Do you remember the golden light that surrounded us just as we came?"

He heard her suck in her breath. "That was the Claiming?"

He looked into her eyes and nodded, holding his breath all the while. This was the part that scared the crap out of him. She could reject him utterly at this point, deny the mating and pull away from him. He wouldn't be too surprised if she did. In the grand scheme of things, they'd only really known each other for three days. Although she wouldn't really be able to go very far, now that the ritual was halfway done.

He watched her absorb the implications. "Do you choose your mate, or is it a fate kind of thing?"

He was surprised. He thought she'd have more questions about the Claiming. "The gods choose our mate for us before we're even born. If we're extremely lucky, we find her or him during the current life; if not, we hope, no, pray we may find them in the next."

"So, there's no choice?"

He didn't like the slow, considering way she said that. "The moment I saw you, no other woman would do. Before the other night, do you know how long it had been since I'd had sex?"

"No."

"A year."

She blinked, stunned. "A year?"

"You went seven." His grin was lopsided, he knew, but this was too important an issue to screw up with a lame joke.

Dare to Believe

"But…your reputation…the blondes you escorted all over the place…"

"I dated, occasionally, but I didn't really…click…with anyone. Couldn't figure out why, at first."

"You joined the company five years ago."

He nodded, watching the wheels turn in his woman's head.

"But we didn't meet until three days ago."

His expression turned tender. "Vanilla and peaches."

"Huh?"

"Your scent. Vanilla and peaches. I could smell it wherever I went in the company. Took me a while to track it down to accounting, and when I finally did I had the CEO slot, and you kept disappearing." She bit her lip, looking guilty. "Yeah, I figured it was deliberate." He sighed. "I could see you occasionally from the back, and, while I must say it is a mighty fine view, I prefer the one from the front." He brushed a hand down her cheek, delighted when she blushed. "I love watching your eyes."

Those beautiful eyes of hers darkened, as did the blush that still stained her cheeks. "When…" she cleared her throat, "…when did you realize I was yours?"

Leo resisted the urge to grin in triumph. She'd accepted him, whether it was consciously done or not. "When I tasted you."

"What?"

"Remember the kiss on the dance floor at the Halloween party?"

"The one where you tried to lick my toes through my mouth?"

He laughed. "Has anyone told you that you have an interesting way with words?"

"Mm-hmm. Was that when?"

"Yes. I knew you were the one for me." He couldn't help himself. He stroked her hair back from her cheek, enjoying the feel of it slipping through his fingers. Everything about her fascinated him.

"This whole bonding thing. What's the next step?"

He returned his gaze to her face. "The next step is the actual ceremony. In it I pledge my being to you, and I share of my power with you. In doing so, I grant you some of my life force, which lengthens your life. You'll live as long as I do, actually. It's one of the true pieces of magic the Sidhe actually possess, other than our human glamour. All Fae have a human seeming. It's a gift from the gods to protect us in the human world."

"And the whole *Arabian Nights* slash *Easy Rider* thing wasn't magic?"

He shook his head. "Not like other Fae can do, like my Dad."

"Sean isn't Sidhe?"

He sighed and took her hand, just because. He began stroking her fingers absently. "No, he's not, and that's the root of a lot of the problems on the Joloun side. His blood isn't blue enough for Mom's family to fully accept him."

"What kind of Fae is he, then?"

He looked at her and just *knew* what her reaction was going to be. "He's a leprechaun."

For a moment she didn't react. Then her lips twitched.

"I wouldn't say it if I were you."

If she heard the mild warning in his voice she chose to ignore it. "So, are they really always after his Lucky Charms?" Her eyes were beginning to water as she tried to suppress her laugh.

"Ruby, I'd stop now." He could feel Sean beginning to move towards the barn. When a leprechaun wanted to, he could move with preternatural speed on his own land.

"Can I see the purple horseshoes?" She bit her lip, the laugh beginning to escape.

His father was inside the barn now, propped up against the door, one ankle crossed over the other to match the arms crossed over his chest. He was staring up at the hayloft with an amused expression. Leo sighed.

"So, is the blue moon this month?"

Sean's brow rose and Leo braced himself. "No, but I understand the two of you were mooning my horses a little while ago. Care to come down here and ask *me* those questions now?"

Ruby jumped, her face filled with a mixture of guilt and fun.

"Dad, we're not bonded yet, so don't do anything... permanent, okay?"

Ruby leaned over the side and grinned down at Sean. "So, what *really* happens if I take my eyes off the leprechaun?"

Leo's awed, horrified "*Holy shit!*" was almost lost as Sean gave her a wickedly lethal grin. "Darling, if you're really, *really* lucky, said leprechaun will show you he knows *exactly* where the pot of gold is."

Leo gaped. He knew his father was devoted to his mother. He also knew his father wouldn't *really* put the moves on Ruby. When his father winked at him, he closed his mouth.

Sometimes Leo needed that little reminder that, in fact, *he* was a leprechaun, too.

Sean pushed away from the doorframe. "Now, if you two are

done playing in my hayloft, Aileen has lunch ready." Sean sauntered, whistling, towards the house, and Leo's heart left his throat.

"You are a brave, brave woman, and if you ever scare me like that again I will tie you up and lock you in a tower for the rest of your life."

Ruby looked back at him. Something in his face must have given away exactly how much she'd frightened him, because now, after the fact, she looked concerned. "What?"

Leo took a steady, calming breath. She had to learn, and she had to learn fast. He couldn't let her be hurt through ignorance. "Leprechauns are earth spirits. This is Dad's land. If he really wanted to, he could hear a whisper a mile away, cause an earthquake, open a sinkhole the size of a dime that goes damn near to the core of the earth, you name it. He knows everything that happens on his land unless something is done deliberately to block him. The minute you started with the jokes he knew and headed over here." Leo growled. *And you are very lucky he likes you.*"

"Oh."

"Needless to say, we did not eat Lucky Charms when I was a kid."

"Poor deprived baby." The joke was almost absent-minded, like she'd already dismissed his warning. "Lunch, then we finish the conversation?"

His stomach growled.

She laughed shakily and tugged him to his feet. "C'mon, big guy, let's go eat."

Jaden slammed the drawer shut with a snarl. The damn

bitch was getting loonier by the day, and if he didn't find out how she'd figured out his weakness soon he was going to scream.

Jaden paced the room, knowing he had about an hour before the Deranged Darling got back from her big society party. She'd hopped Daddy's jet for a little jaunt to California yesterday, and Jaden for one couldn't be happier.

Jaden hoped she got hit by a bus. It wouldn't kill her, but damn if it wouldn't make *him* feel better.

She was so meticulous and neat, she had to have the information written down somewhere. But it wasn't in her desk, her room, or in the hidden safe behind the Renoir, and damn if that wasn't one of the cheesiest things he'd ever seen. Talk about a cliché.

Where would she hide it? If he could just lay his hands on the name of the person who ratted him out…

Not Duncan. Not after everything they'd been through together. Duncan had taken a frightened newbie vamp in, one who'd been tossed out by his Master, and helped him find his feet and fangs in a world where vamps were the lowest rung of the social ladder.

Oh, sure, if you were a Black Court vamp you were pretty high on the food chain. Of course, if you remained Black Court after being turned it pretty much guaranteed you were a psychotic ass-hat. White Court, on the other hand, looked down on vamps as lower than dog shit until you proved, beyond a shadow of a doubt, that you could overcome the Dark Queen's taint. Jaden held back a cynical laugh. Like he had a choice about being "tainted". For the White Court, proving you were untainted usually meant being dead. A dead vamp was the best vamp, as far as Queen Glorianna was concerned. It was why most vamps who left the Black Court pledged their allegiance to

Oberon and the Gray Court. There vamps were treated just like any other fae. If you fucked up, the Court fucked you up. If you didn't, you lived a happy, productive life. It was something Jaden could understand, even encourage. He'd sent more than one lost young vamp to Oberon's mountain palace.

When they first met, Duncan had looked past the fact that Jaden hadn't yet pledged himself to Oberon. Duncan had seen Jaden, and liked something in him. He'd taken him in, made him his right-hand man. Hell, he'd fucking blood-bonded with him, even if it was only the lightest bond a vampire could cast. To be bonded to a White Court Sidhe lord was almost unheard of for one of his kind. He'd been Duncan's ever since.

And if it wasn't for the fact that the Deranged Darling was Duncan's family she'd already be dead.

Jaden stomped out of the office, closing the door behind him and relocking it quickly. She'd never know he'd been there. He'd long since learned the knack of searching without leaving a trace. He headed to his own office, located right next to Duncan's, and slumped into his chair. He put his feet up on his desk, tipped his head back, and tried to come up with a plan that would free him from Kaitlynn without losing the one person on the face of the earth Jaden would gladly die for.

Ruby spent lunch mostly absorbing what Leo had told her in the hayloft. The part that wasn't trying to understand everything she'd been shown was enjoying the look of shock and awe on Moira's face all through the meal. She kept darting glances between Ruby and her father, and Sean knew exactly what his daughter was doing. He kept his face serene, but when Moira wasn't looking he winked at Ruby.

After the meal, Ruby turned to Aileen. "Is there anything I

need to know about a Sidhe mating that Leo might not want me to know?"

"Hey!"

Ruby ignored Leo's indignant shout and focused all of her attention on Aileen.

Aileen stared at her thoughtfully. "What has he told you so far?"

Ruby recounted everything Leo had told her, leaving out the incredibly hot sex they'd engaged in, but from the small smile on Aileen's face she had the feeling Sean had already filled her in on that small fact.

"So. You know how the Claiming is done, starting with tasting and ending in...hmmm... I believe you understand that part just fine." Aileen smiled serenely at her son, who flushed bright red. "The Vow is quite simple, really."

Turning to Sean, Aileen took his hands in her own. "I vow that from this day forward you shall not walk alone. My strength is your protection, my heart is your shelter, and my arms are your home. I shall serve you in all those ways that you require. I pledge to you my living and my dying, each equally in your care. Yours is the name I whisper at the close of each day and the eyes into which I smile each morning. I give you all that is mine to give. My heart and my soul I pledge to you. You are my Chosen One, you are my mate, and you are bound to me for eternity."

Sean kissed the back of Aileen's hand, the love he felt for his petite wife very evident. "I vow that from this day forward you shall not walk alone. My strength is your protection, my heart is your shelter, and my arms are your home. I shall serve you in all those ways that you require. I pledge to you my living and my dying, each equally in your care. Yours is the name I whisper at the close of each day and the eyes into which I smile each morning. I give you all that is mine to give. My heart and my soul I pledge to you. You are my Chosen One, you are my mate, and you are bound to me for eternity."

Ruby sighed. "That's beautiful."

Aileen turned to her, her face still glowing with her love for her husband. "That's the Vow. There's a bit more to it than that, a flow of magic that's exchanged when two people take the Vow. That's called the Binding."

"But I'm human, I don't possess magic."

"Oh, yes you do, kitten." Ruby turned to find Leo watching her, that quiet possessiveness once again in evidence. "All humans have magic, they just don't know how to find it."

"I don't know if I understand." Ruby stared into Leo's otherworldly face, knowing her confusion showed by the concern in his expression. He hadn't bothered to put his glamour back up.

"Trust me, kitten. Okay? Without speaking the Vow there's no way to demonstrate the Binding, and since my parents are already bonded they can't show you what it looks like."

She sighed. "I've trusted you since the party, so I guess I can keep going out on that particular limb."

Leo picked up her hand and placed a gentle kiss on the back of her fingers. "The only possibly frightening part for you would be if the Binding is strong enough to have visible results."

"Like the Claiming?"

Leo shot his parents a quick look. "Not quite. If the Vow is taken during a time of stress it's possible the show would be a bit more spectacular than that."

"Oh." Ruby thought the Claiming light show was spectacular. What would be next, fireworks? "What's the third part of the mating again?"

"There's the Claiming, the Vow, and the Binding."

Her head was beginning to spin. She got the Claiming and the Vow, but... "What's the Binding again?"

"That's the part where my power and yours blend, bonding us together for eternity."

Oh. "Eternity is a really long time, Leo."

"No. It's not. Eternity is looking for your soul mate and never finding her."

Leo used the hand he was holding to pull her to her feet. "We'll be in our room."

Leo closed the door and turned to face his reluctant mate. "Okay, kitten, now you know."

"You're positive I'm yours?"

Leo nodded, his eyes never leaving her face. Her face was shadowed, her brows drawn together in a thoughtful frown. She licked her lips and drew a quick breath. "How does this affect Shane's kidnapping?"

"If the Malmaynes have their way, our mating would be set aside in favor of the alliance marriage, something I'm not willing to risk."

"How can a mating be set aside? I kind of thought that was permanent?"

"Our mating isn't complete. They could say that I could fulfill the terms of the contract and then return to you. Of course, Sidhe breeding being what it is, odds are you'd be around seventy years old before Kaitlynn conceived."

"Seventy..." Her awed whisper tapered off into a low whistle. "And you'd still be..." She waved her hand in his direction. He could only assume what she meant.

"Young? Yeah, pretty much."

Her "hmph" was thoughtful. "But, if they won't accept Shane or Moira as a substitute..." She huffed out a breath and began pacing, growing agitated. "I mean, why does it have to be you?"

"Because my magic is almost pure Sidhe. Moira's is almost pure leprechaun and Shane... Well, we're still not quite certain how to classify Shane, other than wild."

Ruby cocked her head, more confused than ever. "Wild?"

"The Sidhe and leprechaun blood in Shane is almost evenly mixed. He has the powers of both, with a little extra something genetics seems to have thrown into the mix."

"What would that be?"

Leo shrugged. "If Shane exerts himself, using both his leprechaun and Sidhe powers in tandem, he can make fantasy reality."

"You mean he could actually make that tent appear?"

"The harem tent? Yes, down to the outfit you were wearing."

"Wow," she breathed, intrigued at the possibilities.

"He uses it mostly in his work. He's an artist."

Her eyes went wide with admiration. "Wait. Your brother is Shane Joloun?" When he nodded, she whistled again.

Leo moved, pulling her against him. His hands cupped her ass, kneading it leisurely. "I wouldn't even think of it, Ruby. You'll find you have a very jealous mate."

She looked up at him, her eyes twinkling. "You don't want the houri outfit? I want your harem pants, oh sheik!"

Leo leaned down and kissed her, hard and swift.

"How does he do it?"

Dare to Believe

His lips had barely left hers before the question popped out. "We're not sure, but we think it's the earth sprite part. The tent would be made of silk, like the pillows, both born of the earth. Add in that he could read the fantasy in your head, and bingo! Instant harem tent." Leo continued to knead her ass, loving the feeling of the firm globes under his hands. "But he can't do it very often. It tires him out pretty quickly, so he usually uses it for self-defense, work, or sex."

"*Sex*? You mean, he makes his fantasies realities and—"

Leo laughed. "No! We can't make life, Ruby! We're not gods, after all."

"Then what—"

"Condoms."

Ruby just stared at him for a moment, looking disgusted and amused. "Your brother has the power of limited creation in his hands, and he uses it to make Trojans. What, he doesn't know where the drug store is?" Leo's cheeks flushed and he laughed, knowing he looked guilty as hell. Her eyes narrowed. "You talked him into that one, didn't you?"

"Gee, is that a car I hear in the driveway? I wonder who it could be?" Leo smiled falsely and dove for the window. Any sense of fun dissolved two seconds later. "Fuck. That's unexpected."

"What?"

Leo turned around. "The Malmaynes are here."

Ruby stood at Leo's side and watched the Malmaynes step out of the limousine. The first out was an attractive older gentleman, his white blond hair lightly sprinkled with silver. His dark blue eyes were cold and arrogant. He took in his surroundings with the air of someone who smelled something foul. His body was lean and tall in his expensive gray designer suit.

The vision that stepped out of the limo behind him made Ruby want to crawl back into the house. She looked very familiar. The young woman she'd once seen Leo escorting around town was peachy perfection. Her white gold hair and gray eyes shone with an unearthly beauty Ruby could never hope to match. Her dress, a pale pink satin, showed off her milky cleavage without being vulgar. The hemline ended just above the knee showing just the right hint of leg. Her pale pumps and clutch bag finished the outfit. Her hair, done up in a neat twist, had just enough escaping tendrils to make the style sleekly sexy. She was a delicate orchid to Ruby's stumpy, common dandelion. She could only be Kaitlynn Malmayne, the woman who wanted to marry Leo.

Leo tucked Ruby beneath his arm protectively as the Malmaynes looked at the Dunnes. Kaitlynn Malmayne's cool expression turned to surprised hurt when she saw how closely Leo held Ruby to his side. She quickly hid the hurt behind disdain, but Ruby saw it, and wondered.

"Leo, did you and she ever…" Ruby whispered as silently as possible.

"No."

"Good."

Leo's quick huff of laughter was quickly masked by a cough.

She watched as Malmayne made his way to Aileen, completely ignoring Sean. "Aileen, it's good to see you, even under the circumstances."

Aileen ignored the hand the man held out. "The circumstances are completely of your making, Cullen. Give me back my son."

Cullen Malmayne sneered. "Charming as ever, my dear." Once again completely ignoring Sean, Cullen moved to Leo. "Leo. Good to see you."

Leo nodded coldly. "Wish I could say the same, Cullen. Now give me back my brother."

Cullen's sneer warmed, his eyes roaming Ruby's curves. "And who is this young lady? A friend of yours?"

Leo's smile was smug. "She's my mate."

Cullen's warm smile dropped into an icy glare. He studied Ruby coldly, with thinly veiled disgust. Behind him, Kaitlynn gasped. "The binding is incomplete." He sniffed and turned back to Leo. "Fulfill the Joloun end of the agreement and I'll see to it your brother is returned to you unharmed."

"No."

Cullen sighed and shook his head. "I don't see that you have any choice, Leo. Without your cooperation the deal becomes null and void, and the Joloun family suffers. Is it your wish to see your mother suffer, or your sister? How about Shane, Leo? Do you wish to see him suffer any further?"

Leo's expression turned into a shark's grin that sent a shiver down Ruby's spine. "First, I don't believe there was a time limit to the contract, was there, Malmayne?" When Cullen didn't respond beyond a rising of his eyebrows, Leo continued. "Second, it merely said that the partners be descendants of either you or Duncan, and my mother or her descendants. Since both my brother and sister are descendants of my mother, perhaps you'd care to approach one of them to fulfill your contract? I'm afraid I'm unavailable."

Cullen shook his head almost sadly, his cold gaze firmly on Leo. "Unacceptable. Your sister's and brother's blood is too polluted to be of use to me. Yours, on the other hand, is nearly pure."

Leo's smile became sharper, harder at the insult to his family. "Yours, on the other hand, is pure liquid shit."

Ruby heard the vague hint of an Irish brogue in Leo's voice.

Cullen sighed.

All of Ruby's most shameful nightmares came out of the corners of her mind and began to attack her. Her insecurities crowded around her in a kaleidoscope of pain and anguish that sent her straight to her knees with a whimper.

"*Ruby is such a lousy fuck!*" Bobby Pencil-Dick's voice sneered in her ears as he told all of his friends about her. "*Man, if that's what doing a virgin is like I'll stick with the bitches who know what a blowjob is.*" But this time, she wasn't able to fight back.

"*She's so fat she's just jiggling in that dress. Watch it wiggle, see it jiggle...*" The giggles of the cheerleaders surrounded her. They sang that hated jingle, pointing and laughing at Ruby. It had taken her years to get to the size she was now, but none of that mattered as it all came rushing back, the emotions as strong as they'd been at the time it had happened.

"*You know, you'd be so much more attractive if you'd just lose ten pounds, sweetheart. Now, if you follow this diet I've laid out for you...*" Her mother's voice drifted away, her father's taking its place. "*Baby girl, if you don't put that cake down you're going to weigh more than an elephant!*" The laughter of all of her cousins, uncles and aunts mingled with the giggles of the cheerleaders. What made it worse was her parents didn't even realize how badly they'd hurt her. They'd thought they were helping.

"*Don't know what makes you think you can make it in college. It's not like you have a brain in your head.*" Cousin Trina's voice made her cringe; her brain had been her only asset all through school. "*Course, with hooters like yours, who needs* brains?"

It's not real, it's not real, it's not real. She chanted the mantra in her head, not that it did much good. This Malmayne-induced nightmare continued on and on until Ruby thought she'd begin screaming for real.

And then she saw it, the light at the end of the high school corridor. A figure stood there, vaguely familiar, strong and confident. He held out one hand to her, beckoning her to him. All she had to do was have the courage to go to him. But how could she walk that gauntlet with all of those eyes staring at her?

Besides, he was a young god, so good looking it made her heart hurt just to look at him. He couldn't possibly be there for her.

But somehow she knew he was. Glowing peridot eyes pulled at her. His black hair hung to his shoulders, longer than she thought it was supposed to be, but she still couldn't remember why he looked so familiar to her. He wore black leather pants that hugged his legs in a way that should be outlawed. His black T-shirt clung lovingly to every muscle, looking almost painted on. He wore a gold ring on the hand he held out to her, with some sort of dark stone in the center.

That stone sent a flash of memory through her. She knew the initials *RH* were carved in the face of the stone. Her initials.

He was hers.

Without thinking about it, she reached up to feel the collar that should encircle her own neck. With a satisfied smile she felt it, the relief that it was there, branding her, almost overwhelming. The mocking, sometimes painfully loving, voices of everyone else faded away until she could only hear *his* voice.

"Come to me, kitten." When she hesitated, he growled, "You know you're meant to ride off with me. You belong to me."

Ruby looked down, not surprised to see the leather halter top and leather pants. She smiled, feeling warm and sexy, no longer aware of anything but him. Leo. She worked her way down the corridor, showing off her own leathers to the best of her ability, but it wasn't for those who had once caused her so much pain.

It was all for him.

Then she slipped her hand into his and stepped into the sunshine. She blinked dazedly as she realized she was back on the Dunne farm.

She gasped as her hand was yanked viciously out of Leo's, her body tugged away from him. "I don't think so, *human.*" Cullen Malmayne pulled her behind him, away from Leo, totally ignoring her struggles.

Apparently Sidhe lords are really friggin' strong, she thought, tugging harder on her hand. No matter how hard she pulled she didn't even slow Cullen down. He just barreled forward, her struggles barely registering to him.

She heard a strange roaring sound behind her. The ground beneath her feet began to tremble. Turning in Cullen's suddenly lax grasp, she saw Leo in his full, furious glory.

Multicolored strands of light whipped around his body in a strangely erotic, lethal dance. Ruby suspected that if anyone attempted to touch Leo in that moment they would die a grisly death. He glared at Cullen Malmayne, his human seeming gone. His eyes glowed even brighter in his fury, his hair blowing about in a nonexistent breeze. Leo looked furious at the sight of her in Malmayne's hands.

"Ruby is *my mate* and *no one* will take her from me!"

Ruby gasped at the power in Leo's voice. The earth bucked up between her and Cullen, forcing Cullen to release her arm as they fought for balance.

Leo began stalking towards her, his light reaching out to encircle her, pushing Cullen and the others away from her in a possessive, protective display that dazzled her. She backed up, her eyes wide as he kept pace with her, his glowing gaze never leaving her face.

"I vow that from this day forward you shall not walk alone."

"NO, Leo!" Cullen's voice cut across the wind, surprisingly clear. "Kaitlynn—"

"My strength is your protection, my heart is your shelter, and my arms are your home." Leo ignored the Malmayne patriarch, his eyes only for his mate, the hint of Irish brogue telling her exactly how upset he was. "I shall serve you in all of those ways that you require. I pledge to you my living and my dying, each equally in your care." Ruby could feel his power wrapping around her, leaving her breathless. The warm caress of it was like sunlight on a summer's day. He reached out with one hand to cup her cheek, his power wrapping around her like a familiar, comforting blanket. That was when she realized it wouldn't hurt her. "Yours is the name I whisper at the close of each day and the eyes into which I stare each morning."

"Stop it, Leo!" Ruby looked to see who had yelled and saw Kaitlynn, her big gray eyes swimming with tears. "You are promised to me!"

Leo ignored the other woman, his gaze never leaving Ruby's face. "I give you all that is mine to give. My heart and my soul I pledge to *you*." He lifted his other hand to cradle her face between them. "*You* are my Chosen One." Kaitlynn cried out, the sound full of despair. "You are my Mate, and you are bound to me for eternity."

The bands of light surrounding Leo reared back, then speared into Ruby's body in a rush so dizzying she felt faint. She could feel the joining of their souls as Leo's magic filled every cell in her body. The rush of power tingled along every part of her, pushing her into one of the most intense orgasms of her life. She shuddered in his arms, too breathless to scream. When he kissed her it merely added another dimension to the already painful pleasure coursing through her. Darkness washed over her in a rippling tide, pulling her under. The magic gradually left her body, and with it, consciousness.

Leo caught her before she fell very far, scooping her limp form up into his arms with a worried frown. "Mom!"

"Give her to me, son." Sean held his arms out and Leo handed his truebond over, knowing his father would die himself before allowing his daughter-in-law to come to harm. He watched his father carry Ruby into the house, ignoring the Malmaynes until the door shut behind them.

With the remnants of the Bonding power still whipping around him he turned to face the Malmaynes. His slow smile of satisfaction was cold as he and Cullen faced one another. "The ritual is complete, and it's True. Not even Oberon himself could set it aside."

He watched Cullen take a deep, shaken breath. Such a powerful bonding was impossible for the other Sidhe lord to deny. "So it would seem." Cullen turned to Kaitlynn, who hadn't moved since her aborted attempt to halt Leo's bonding. "My dear, perhaps you should reconsider Shane."

Her damp blue eyes turned to her father. "I want Leo."

Cullen sighed. "Kaitlynn, I'm afraid that's no longer possible."

"But I want Leo."

Leo frowned at the quiet desperation in her voice. Though he didn't know Kaitlynn well, he did know her. Did she harbor feelings for him he was unaware of? If so, he pitied her. His body, heart, and soul were currently in his parents' house being tended to by his father.

"Leo is unavailable, obviously." Cullen ran his hand down her arm, trying to soothe his daughter. "Shane is not unattractive."

She yanked her arm away from him. "Shane is a freak. I don't want Shane. I want Leo."

Leo bristled at hearing his brother labeled a freak. "Then perhaps you'd be so kind as to return him to us?" He could still hear the brogue in his voice and deliberately coarsened it, thickened it until it rivaled his father's.

Kaitlynn looked at him, her expression turning to sly calculation. "There are situations in which a truebond and an alliance marriage have been co-arranged. Perhaps we should consider that."

"No."

Kaitlynn flinched at the hard finality of his tone. "Why not? It would solve the problem of the marriage contract and give us both what we want."

"I am bonded already, Kaitlynn. Even if I wished to, my body is bound to Ruby's. I couldn't even if I wanted to."

"Unless she wanted you to."

Leo stared at her, wondering what in hell was going through her mind now. Ruby would *never* be willing to share him, even if he was willing to allow it.

"Think about it, Leo. You could have both of us, legally, and satisfy the terms of the agreement. Ruby and I could fulfill every fantasy you've ever had. And she wouldn't need much persuasion, human that she is. All it would take is a little magic." Kaitlynn tried to lay a hand on his arm, no doubt to entice him. Enough of the binding energy still surrounded him, however, that her hand got no closer than an inch before she pulled it back with a cry of pain. "Damn it to hell!" Angry red spots appeared on her fingertips as she hunched over her hand.

Leo shrugged. "I told you. My bondmate doesn't like to share." Leo stepped back, putting some distance between him and the seething woman before him. "And neither do I."

"We'll see about that." Cullen totally forgotten, Leo stared at the woman he was rapidly coming to realize was his true adversary. She straightened up, a slow, sleepy smile crossed her face. "Perhaps I can change your mind."

"I don't think so." Leo's gaze was steady. He watched her smooth the skirt of her dress, her poise once more in place.

"We'll see." She turned to Cullen, her eyes once again serene. "Father?"

Cullen moved towards his daughter and assisted her into the limousine. "Leo. A pity we won't be adding you to our family roster."

"Pardon me if I find myself grateful for the reprieve."

Cullen's sour smile was his only answer. The Malmaynes drove away from the farm, leaving him with a new problem. How was he going to explain what had happened to Ruby? Bonding her had been instinct, the sight of Cullen dragging Ruby away, hurting her, more than he could bear. He turned back to the house, the sight of his mother in the doorway bringing him up short.

"Damn it." Leo sighed as he realized they hadn't promised to return Shane.

It wasn't over. Not by a long shot.

Chapter Seven

Jaden Blackthorn was having one of the best nights of his life. He watched the security monitor, nearly cackling with glee. This was better than Buffy reruns. Better than sex!

Scratch that. Even Kaitlynn's failure and ultimate humiliation isn't...

Never mind. This is *better than sex.*

Shane Joloun was making a break for it, and fairly successfully, too. The reason it was so successful was the two guards who were supposed to be monitoring Shane's cell, weren't.

Shane had managed to conjure up a tire iron and wasn't afraid to use it. Cold iron in a Sidhe household could be a real bitch. Oddly, the hybrid didn't seem to be affected by it at all. He was dressed in the dark blue silk Jaden had seen him summon. With leather-soled shoes on his feet he made barely a sound. The hybrid ghosted through the corridors of Malmayne House, taking out anyone who made the mistake of getting in his way.

He winced with faux sympathy as Shane cold-cocked another guard, turning the poor man's already muddy brains to pure mush.

Cullen and Kaitlynn were going to be *so* pissed when they got home. And Jaden hadn't had to do a thing other than be quiet. And make sure the power went out on the whole block. Oh, and knock the stupid security guards in the control room out with a tire iron after kicking the door in. Funny, that; using cold iron really didn't bother vampires. Something the Deranged Darling should keep in mind for the next time she threatened him, if he let her *have* a next time.

Hell, by the time the emergency generator had kicked in, Shane was halfway out of the house.

Jaden kept his thoughts, and his eyes, glued to the monitor and nearly crowed with glee. Beating the two guards and watching the hybrid work had been pure pleasure. Listening to Kaitlynn's frustrated screams would be icing on the cake.

He stayed long enough to make sure Shane got off the grounds before leaving the security area the way he'd come. He made it back to his room unnoticed by any of the surviving guards. Settling back down on his bed, he finally allowed the laughter he'd been holding back free rein.

Then, hungry, he went out for a bite to eat. He decided on a blonde, finding a lovely little piece of ass just wandering, slightly drunk, out of a bar. He followed her down the street, ready to pull her into a dark alley...

The knife at his throat didn't scare him. The voice, however, did. "Hello, Jaden."

He swallowed, terrified, as the slender man pulled him into the alleyway. He knew better than to fight. "Hob."

He bit back a cry as he was slammed, hard, to the ground. Tendrils of...*something*, broke the concrete pavement to wrap around his body, piercing his skin and pinning him in place through the arms, legs, and abdomen. The pain was excruciating. They pinned him to the ground and he screamed, but he made no sound. The Hob had muffled it.

He looked up through tear-drenched eyes to see the Hob

smiling down at him. "Where's Shane Joloun Dunne?" The Hob asked Jaden the question in the same tone of voice someone would ask where the bathroom was.

"Gone."

Slender fingers, tipped in black claws, gripped his chin. "Don't lie to me, Jaden. Not to me. I don't like it when people do that."

"He's gone!"

One slender black claw began tapping against his cheek. "Really?"

He sobbed as the tendrils in his body pulsed, pouring poison into his system, ratcheting the pain up to nearly unbearable levels.

"I'm going to ask you again. Where is Shane Dunne?"

"Gone!"

The Hob shook his head, his eyes closing. "Oh, Jaden. And you were one of my best." He tsk'd before opening his eyes to reveal Hell.

By the time the screaming died down to low whimpers the Hob had all the answers he needed.

Robin stared down at the sweaty and blood-soaked vampire on the ground. He actually felt some remorse for what he'd done to the man, but he had to be sure Jaden was telling the truth.

He *hadn't* lied, and now Robin owed him. And the Hob *always* paid his debts.

He started by removing all of Jaden's memories from the point he'd taken him. No need for him to remember what had been done to him. The wounds would heal on their own. Given enough time, the poisons would pass, the fractures would mend, the cuts and bruises disappearing after a good feeding. But time wasn't something Jaden had at the moment. If Kaitlynn got her hands on him in this condition, the vampire didn't stand a chance. And that would be Robin's fault.

With a sigh the Hob slit his wrist and held it, dripping, to the vampire's mouth. "Debt repaid."

He deemed it enough when Jaden's body began to glow. He was gone in a swirl of dust and wind before Jaden even had a chance to regain consciousness.

Leo stared down at Ruby, sleeping so peacefully in his bed. She was curled up on her side, her breathing deep and even.

He swallowed. He couldn't shake off the terror. "It's been two days. She hasn't woken up. Not once."

His mother rested her hand on his shoulder. "Give it time, Leo. It was a very powerful bonding."

"What if it was too much for her? What if she never wakes up?" He ran his fingers through Ruby's hair, willing her to wake up.

"She'll wake up."

He sat on the edge of the bed, unable to leave his mate's side even for a moment. "Has a human ever survived a bond this strong?"

His mother's moment of silence only deepened his fear. "Her body is changing, Leo. Her energies are aligning with yours. She'll share your lifespan. Some sleep is normal."

"This much sleep?" He looked up at his mother, pleading with her to reassure him.

Aileen looked away, her eyes closing in pain.

Leo closed his own and prayed.

She'll be all right. She has to be. Lord, please let her be all right.

Ruby sighed. She tugged at the comforter, frowning when Leo's butt kept it from moving very far.

Leo jumped up, watching with joy as Ruby snuggled under the comforter. She pulled it up to her chin and settled back down.

He allowed his mother to tug him from the room. "Wake her in a few hours, Leo." She grinned up at him, some of the worries of the last few days leaving her face. "And then wake her properly."

He leaned down and kissed his mother's cheek. "I will. Thank you, Mom."

She nodded and left him to watch over his wife.

The scent of fresh-brewed manna from heaven wafted by her on the morning breeze.

"If you don't wake up, I'll drink your coffee."

The demon's threat filtered down into her caffeine-deprived brain and she groaned. One hand lifted weakly in the direction the wonderful aroma was coming from.

"That's it, kitten, open those pretty brown eyes."

The demon was laughing at her. Ruby opened one weary eye and glared blearily up at the Evil One. She closed her eyes and groaned.

She could hear him blowing. The scent of the coffee went straight to her nose and filtered into her brain. "Cooo-fffeeeeee. C'mon, kitten, you can do it for coffee, right?"

"Gimme." She lurched up and grabbed the mug, downing the entire contents in one very long pull, ignoring the sting of heat. She then, very precisely, put the mug on the end table and collapsed, all without opening her eyes. She pulled her pillow over her head. "Go 'way."

Okay. The demon was definitely laughing at her. "If you get up I can get you more coffee."

She pulled her head out from under the pillow and glared at him some more. "Promise?"

"Promise."

She sighed, her natural sense of humor waking up. The caffeine moving through her system didn't hurt, either. "Okay, fine, I'm up." After a long, languid, full-body stretch she sat up, running her fingers through her tousled hair.

Leo wasn't laughing any more. His gaze was riveted to her body, watching her stretch with a hungry expression. With a start she realized what kind of a show she was giving him. She also realized for the first time that she was stark naked.

"Oh, no. No, no, no. Not before two cups of coffee, at least."

"How about a good morning kiss then?"

"Hmmm. All right, seeing as you brought me my coffee." Ruby screwed her eyes shut and pursed her lips, waiting for his.

She waited.

And waited.

Finally she opened one eye. "What?" she said from between her still puckered lips.

"You're kidding me, right?"

She bit her lip and tried to look innocent. "No. You asked for a kiss. Did I do it wrong?" She batted her eyelashes and gave him her most fake innocent smile.

"Yes."

When he pounced she was unprepared. In less than a second she was flat on her back and giggling like a mad woman.

Leo grabbed both of her hands and pulled them over her head. He gathered her wrists in one large hand, pinning her in place with his weight. He nudged her legs apart and settled his body between her thighs. With his free hand he cupped her cheek tenderly. "Now, let's see about that good morning kiss, kitten."

She didn't get the sweet good-morning kiss she'd expected. What she got was a great deal more. Leo shifted his hand from her cheek to her hair and, with a gentle tug, pulled at her head until he'd tilted her enough to satisfy him. Her eyes widened at the dominant gesture. His mouth swooped down to hers, his lips parting hers with all the force of an invading conqueror. When she gasped he took advantage of it, parting her mouth even further with his tongue, tasting her in a primal possession that had her nipples hardening in anticipation. His tongue began moving rhythmically, fucking her mouth. She moaned beneath him, all thoughts of playing one game gone, taken over by the thought of playing a much more satisfying game.

The hand in her hair began drifting down, reaching for her breast so slowly she thought she would scream. When he finally palmed the weight of it in his large hand she nearly did scream.

"Mmmm, that's what I call a good morning kiss." He whispered the words across her lips. His thumb strummed over her nipple, teasing it even more erect.

Once again her sense of humor got the better of her. "I don't know. That kind of seemed like an average morning kiss."

One brow rose arrogantly. "Is that so?"

"Mm-hmm. You'll have to work at it to turn it into a *good* morning kiss."

"Oh, a challenge." His whisper was full of dark hunger, and

Ruby shivered, wondering what Pandora's Box she'd just opened. "I wonder what it would take to make it a *great* morning kiss."

She shifted, pulling at her hands. She frowned slightly when Leo didn't let go. "Coffee."

"I don't think coffee is what you need, kitten." His thumb continued to move over her nipple. Ruby decided it was a good thing she didn't sleep in panties, since they would have been soaked by now. Being held down by him felt surprisingly erotic.

Although I might not want to tell the big Neanderthal that. God knows he gets off on hauling me around enough as it is. "Oh, coffee's good. I could *really* use coffee, Leo." She looked up at him with hopeful, innocent eyes, all the while laughing inside.

Ruby shivered again. The heated promise in his eyes and smile said she wasn't going anywhere. "I think I know exactly what you need."

"What's that?" The breathy sound of her voice would have shocked her at any other time. But by then, his hand had left her breast and was easing down the length of her body, sending tiny little shivers of need down her spine.

"I think—" his fingers stroked her lower stomach, tracing an erotic pattern that made her breath hitch, "—you need—" his hand inched its way towards her bared pussy, stroking along the top before delving between the cleft, "—to purr." One finger inserted itself between her wet lips, stroking her clit so softly she sighed. His head dipped towards her mouth, pausing when she licked her kiss-swollen lips. His eyes flared with otherworldly light. "Purr for me, kitten," he breathed into her mouth before claiming it.

The light, teasing flicks of his finger over her clit nearly drove her insane. She writhed beneath him, pulling on her

Dare to Believe

wrists, trying to get closer to those teasing fingers of his. He refused to let her go, careful not to bruise her while holding her where he wanted her. He watched her out of hot, glowing eyes, his glamour dropping away from him completely. She bit her lip and moaned beneath him, eager for more of the pleasure he was giving her.

Ruby stared up into his beautiful, nearly-human eyes and groaned. "Leo, please."

"Leo, please what?" He bent down far enough to brush his lips over hers, a light teasing caress that left her totally unsatisfied.

Ruby shifted, her legs caressing his. The rough texture of his jeans was an erotic counterpoint to her bare, satiny skin. She shivered as his fingers stroked over the entrance to her pussy. She could feel herself growing even wetter as he teased her lower lips.

Ruby decided that two could play at that game. Leaving her hands in his one for now, she began undulating beneath him, beginning an erotic dance designed to set him groaning. She lifted her hips in a silent plea for him to deepen his caresses. She licked the shell of his ear, watching the light in his eyes darken as a shudder racked his body. *Yup, I remembered right. That's a hot spot.* She nipped his earlobe. The groan he let loose was music to her ears.

Leo shifted slightly, his eyes closing to half mast as he leaned down. "Do you trust me?" he whispered in her ear.

Something in his tone of voice, some dark desire she could see in his eyes, made her pause as she seriously considered his words. *Did* she trust him enough to do what she suspected he was going to ask?

Ruby looked up into Leo's glowing eyes and realized, yes, she did trust him or she never would have followed him up to

127

his hotel room that first night, let alone gotten on the plane to Nebraska. "Yes."

The dark grin that crossed his face made her hesitate. "Then don't move."

His commanding tone made her shiver. Whether it was from nerves or arousal, she wasn't sure. "Why not?"

Leo got up from the bed, brushing every inch of his body against hers. With a stern glance he reinforced his order that she not move.

He stood over her, staring down at her nakedness with a hunger she'd never encountered before, even from him. His gaze explored every inch of her body. It took every ounce of willpower she had not to cover herself up with her hands, suddenly shy before the possession in his gaze. She kept her arms extended over her head and was rewarded with his pleased, hungry look. "Very good, kitten." He turned away, moving to his suitcase. She heard a zipper being opened, but decided to remain where she was. She had a feeling that Leo was about to introduce her to a game she'd heard of, but wasn't certain she'd ever try anywhere but in her fantasies.

Looks like Leo is about to turn fantasy into reality. She quivered, anticipation tightening her muscles, her nipples beading in the early morning air.

She heard him rummaging around in the suitcase. Turning her head, she could see it was a smaller suitcase than the one that had held his clothes, and one he hadn't bothered unpacking. She'd wondered at the time what was in it but had decided not to question him on it. She'd assumed it was private.

When he began laying out items on the bed, she realized it was *extremely* private.

The first thing Leo laid on the bed was a black tube. She could clearly make out the word *lube* on it, and shuddered slightly. She couldn't tell if it was fear or excitement that caused the shudder.

The second thing Leo laid on the bed was a peach-colored butt plug.

Okay, now I know what the lube is for. She might be inexperienced, but she wasn't *that* naïve. It was smaller than she thought it would be, and some of her nervousness left her.

Until Leo laid the next butt plug on the bed. This one was black and much wider around, and longer. He held it next to the peach one, giving her a hot look before he turned back to the suitcase and put it back in, a clear warning of what he intended to do to her.

Oh, boy.

The next item he pulled out was a bright red penis with an odd attachment on the front. Ruby stared at it, a nervous giggle nearly escaping her.

A small feather duster was pulled out. "Um, do I get the French maid outfit to go with that?"

Leo looked up from the suitcase. There was no amusement in his eyes. "Shhh. No talking. Not yet."

Ruby opened her mouth to argue, but snapped it shut when Leo glared at her.

He nodded his satisfaction and turned back to the suitcase.

A black paddle joined the feather duster on the bed. Ruby's eyebrows rose alarmingly. *Oh, I don't think so! No way that thing gets anywhere near my ass.*

His lips curved. "What makes you think I'd use it just on your ass?"

Her eyes widened. "No way. You did not just talk to me in my head."

"We're bonded, sweetheart. Of course I can get into that

beautiful head of yours."

A pair of Velcro cuffs, linked by a short chain, joined the paddle and the feather duster. A blindfold was set beside them. Finally, Ruby heard the zipper of the suitcase being closed.

Leo picked up the black cuffs and moved around to Ruby's side of the bed. "Do you know what I'm going to do with these, Ruby?"

Ruby watched Leo's face as his hands caressed the cuffs. She smiled, her lips zipped shut by his order not to speak.

Leo nodded in approval. "Good girl, kitten. You can speak."

"You're going to try to tie my wrists to the bedpost, right?"

Leo looked amused. "What do you mean, try?"

Before she knew it, Leo had placed the first cuff around her wrist. He checked it carefully to make sure it wasn't too tight, a gesture that reassured her that Captain Caveman might be coming out to play but *her* Leo was still there somewhere. "Is this some kind of kinky Sidhe courting thing?"

He looped the other cuff through the posts on the mission-style bed. "Courting's done, time for fucking," Leo muttered, putting the other cuff around her free wrist. He made sure it was comfortable for her, waiting for her okay before moving on.

He stopped, looking down at her. She could tell he loved what he saw as his gaze roamed her naked, trapped form. With a piratical grin he reached over her body and grabbed the blindfold. "I've changed my mind." He gently placed the blindfold over her eyes. "I don't want you to purr, kitten."

With the blindfold on she had no clue what he was about to do next. "What do you want me to do, Leo?"

She felt him leave the bed. She strained to hear him, listening for that tell-tale rustle of denim, but it didn't come.

His whisper, when it came, startled her. He'd leaned over

her without a sound. "I want you to scream."

And with that, Leo began her introduction into a world of sensation she never knew existed.

At first nothing happened. She couldn't see a thing. The blindfold was tight, but not uncomfortable. She realized Leo must have done this many times before, he was so comfortable with it. A small spurt of jealousy hit but she shook it off. Whoever he'd done this with before wasn't there in the bed; she was. She heard the rustle of denim and knew Leo had begun moving around the room. She found her head turning slightly to follow the sounds, wondering what he'd do next.

He could play with her senses, she knew, yet somehow also knew that he wouldn't. That wasn't part of this particular game. The blindfold was enough, at the moment, to have her heart beating in nervous anticipation. And knowing that it was all real this time, that he wasn't inside her head, just made the sensations that much more intense.

When the first whisper-soft touch came she gasped.

The feather duster. It glided across her nipples, teasing her with light brushes against her skin. It glided down her stomach, teasing at her navel before dipping into the vee of her thighs. Slow as molasses it glided back up to tickle the side of her neck as she arched in silent invitation.

Her breath was coming in sighs by the time the feather duster lifted away from her. She didn't protest when Leo lifted her knees and positioned her feet on the bed, her legs spread. She was now open to his gaze.

"Hold still," his dark, smoky whisper sounded in her ear.

The touch of the feather duster followed the command, drifting from her knee to her pussy. It tickled lightly just above her aching clit before gliding down her other thigh to dance on her knee. The sensation was almost too much. "Leo?"

He responded to her whispered plea. "Shh. I'm here, kitten."

His weight settled on the bed at her feet. The feather duster was lifted from her body. She waited for the next touch with breathless anticipation, her nerves stretched taught.

She could almost feel his hot gaze gliding over her. "So pretty." He began to pet her pussy and she arched up against it, her thighs closing, trying to lock him in place. "Such a pretty pussy. Keep your legs spread, kitten." She pushed her knees back into position, opening like a flower to him. "Good girl."

He ran one finger up and down her slit, moistening it in her dew. The mattress dipped, the rustle of his jeans against the sheets indicating that he was moving up from her feet to her side. The feather duster once again began dancing lightly over her nipples. "Maybe we'll get these pierced, kitten. What do you think?"

Shock bowed her back up at the thought of getting her nipples pierced. "Nuh-uh."

Leo laughed, rich and dark, and flicked one finger against her nipple.

A non-existent nipple ring was pulled and twisted, sending spirals of heat straight to her clit. "Are you sure?"

"Uh…" Ruby arched up into the incredibly erotic pain as Leo leaned down and pulled on it with his teeth, catching her nipple and worrying it. "No, no, I think I can live without that," she whimpered. *Pleasure yes, needles no!*

He licked the tiny pain, making her hiss in pleasure. "Pretty little rubies to dance on your skin," he whispered against her, his breath hot on her moist, tight flesh.

"They make those non-pierced, you know." She felt him still above her and damned the blindfold. She didn't know if he was laughing or not, but there was no way in hell anyone was getting near her nipples with a needle. "No. Seriously. I saw them on this website—"

"Ruby?"

"Hmm?" She relaxed. His voice was filled with rueful amusement. The sound of his zipper being pulled down was loud.

"Shut up, sweetheart."

"Um. Okay. But no needles near the nipples, right? I mean, that totally kills the moommmfff..."

A buzzing noise started at the same time Leo slipped his cock between her teeth, rocking back and forth into her mouth. She considered nipping him in protest. The buzzing sound became a vibrating sensation against her clit that sent her arching upwards with a surprised howl of pleasure.

"Like that, do you, kitten?" Leo continued his unhurried pace, his cock shuttling back and forth between her lips. He settled the vibrator between her pussy lips, the sensation almost ticklish. "How about this?"

He leaned over slightly and something soft and round pushed up inside her. *The red penis must be a vibrator.*

"You're going to feel the vibrations even more intensely now, kitten," he whispered as he settled the vibrator deep inside her. Something brushed up against her clit as he began fucking her with it, something that sent delight screaming down her spine. "Those are called the rabbit ears, love. How does it feel?"

She moaned when the "ears" once again brushed her clit.

"Now, don't forget about me, kitten." He grasped the back of her head, angling her mouth where he wanted it. He began fucking in and out of her mouth with increased speed, the hand holding the dildo matching him stroke for stroke. Her hips arched up to meet it, driving it in deeper. She let him know of her pleasure the only way she could, moaning around his iron hard flesh and licking him frantically until he groaned.

With an audible pop he pulled out of her sucking mouth. She felt his mouth brush hers lightly before he began kissing his way down her body, pausing long enough to suck on her sensitive nipples. With a twist of his wrist he ground the ears of the vibrator up against her clit and sent her screaming into her first orgasm.

"Oh, yeah, that's what I like to hear." Leo's satisfied voice held an unmistakable hunger in it. The bed began to jiggle again. She could hear cloth rustling and figured he was finally removing his clothes. Her guess was proven right when she felt his hot skin alongside her own, his hand caressing her still quivering flesh. "So, how do you like the vibrator, kitten?"

She thought about it for all of three seconds before she began purring deep in her throat.

"Oh, kitten, you're in trouble now," he laughed. He reached over her body for something, the bed dipping, her body swaying with his movements. She wished he'd take the blindfold off. "Ready for your next experience?"

Since he'd begun licking her nipples as he asked the question, her only response could be a small moan.

"I'll take that as a yes," he muttered, pulling one tight bud into his mouth and suckling, laving the tip with his tongue until she was writhing on the bed.

She felt him insert the vibrator into her and waited for the delicious sensations to brush her clit again. When those sensations brushed her ass instead, she jerked, not at all certain she liked it.

"Relax for me, kitten. If you don't like it, I promise I'll stop. Only pleasure, love."

"You haven't come yet," she muttered, twisting against the

strange sensations shooting through her anus. The vibrations echoed distantly in her clit. The fake cock inside her vibrated in time to the ears on her anus. She licked her lips, wanting something, anything, to ease the ache building inside her.

"No, I haven't. I'm saving it for something, something special."

She froze. "Special? Should I be afraid?"

He leaned down and kissed her soothingly. "No, sweetheart, nothing to be afraid of." She heard the cap of the lube being flicked open, the plastic sound loud in the air. "I'm just going to get you ready so I can ream your ass, that's all."

He said it so matter-of-factly that it didn't register at first. "Uh, Leo?"

"Hmm?" His voice was distracted as he pulled the fake cock out of her pussy.

"I've never... I mean, I'm not sure..."

"Shhh. I am. Trust me, kitten."

She did trust him, or she wouldn't be tied to the bed. Besides, the vibrations against her anus were beginning to feel good. "I am so going to regret this, aren't I?"

She felt him lean over her body, one slick finger rubbing lube over the pucker of her ass. It glided into her ass, the feeling causing her to clench around him in alarm. "Double-dog dare you."

Aw hell.

Ruby blew out a rough breath. "Fine, shove whatever it is up my ass!"

"You need to relax, Ruby."

"No, actually, I don't." She sniffed, thoroughly miffed. *How could he double-dog dare me on that?*

"Yes, you do, or it will hurt."

She could feel the muffled amusement in his voice as she did her best to do a naked, tied up huff. "Fine, see? All relaxed."

She felt him sigh and still the finger inside her. "I won't hurt you, Ruby."

"What?"

"You don't trust me, not yet, but I swear I will do nothing you don't want. So tell me, kitten. Do you want this?"

She sighed, all her half-fun outrage demolished at the seriousness of his tone. He would stop if she said so. "Leo?"

"Yeah, kitten?"

"I trust you." She forced her body to relax back against the mattress, turning her blind eyes to his voice.

"You sure, kitten? You don't seem particularly enthusiastic about the prospect of anal sex."

She shivered. "Limited experience, remember, Leo? How will I know if I like it if you don't show me?" She could almost feel the wheels turning in his head and shrugged. "Of course, I could go somewhere else for my education."

She could feel the outrage pour off him, even with the blindfold. "Like hell!" His mouth descended on her breast and suckled her fiercely. His finger soon began shuttling in and out of her body as he switched to the other breast. The hand that wasn't busy learning her ass moved to her bare mound, his thumb dipping down to begin massaging her clit.

Very quickly Ruby found her hips moving in time to his strokes as his mouth swooped down on hers in a devouring, conquering kiss. There was nothing gentle in his mouth as he laid claim to hers. A second slicked finger joined the first in her ass, stretching her out as he fucked them ruthlessly in and out of her.

"You are mine," he ground out against her lips, and Ruby

began to realize what her teasing had unleashed. "No one else will touch you. No one else will have you. Do you hear me?"

"Yes, Leo." She reached up and brushed a light kiss against his jaw, instinctively trying to soothe the beast she'd unwittingly unleashed.

"No one will take you from me," he ground out, his voice harsh.

"I won't leave you," she whispered, once again trying to soothe him even as her body began to throb.

"Who do you belong to?" The possessiveness in his voice was darkly thrilling. A third finger began shuttling inside her overheated body. It burned, but that burn quickly turned to a dark pleasure that had her arching up into his hand.

"You, I belong to you Leo!"

His fingers scissored open, stretching her, preparing her for what he wanted. He pulled his hands from her body and she cried out, feeling empty. Once again the bed dipped as he reached over her body, his hard and taught above hers, and heard the clack of the plastic lid of the lube being opened. She heard him squelch the lube over something and hoped to God it wasn't his cock. She wasn't certain she was ready for that.

"Hold still, kitten." She felt him begin to thrust something much larger than his fingers into her ass and consciously relaxed her muscles, pushing out against the invasion. The butt plug slipped in with surprising ease, the pleasure mingling with the slight pain as the fat base slipped past her muscles to fit snuggly inside her.

"You did beautifully, kitten," he whispered against her lips as he positioned his body above hers. "You are so gorgeous with that plug up your ass."

She felt his cock at the entrance of her pussy and her eyes widened behind the blindfold. She felt full just from the butt plug. How the hell was he going to fit that monster in, as well?

She opened her lips to protest when she felt the head of his cock slip into her pussy. He pushed inside her in a slow, inexorable slide, the satin-smooth iron bar of flesh parting her, and she choked on her words at the feeling.

She'd never felt so full in her life. It was almost more than she could bear.

And then he began to move.

He began fucking her slowly at first, letting her feel the full slide of him as he pulled out, the gentle push as he reentered her body. She could feel him against the butt plug, such a tight fit she was surprised the flesh between her pussy and ass didn't rupture.

When he flipped the switch on the butt plug and made it begin to vibrate, she screamed.

Faster and faster he fucked in and out of her body. She could feel his sweat dripping down onto her. He whispered to her in that sweet lilting language she didn't understand. He began pounding into her as the vibrations in her ass intensified, shuddering in and out of her body so hard she could hear their flesh slapping together.

And she loved every fucking minute of it.

The man of her dreams was fucking her into the mattress, pounding his body against hers, losing that tight control he usually kept on himself. She threw her hips up at him, matching him stroke for stroke, brushing her clit against the base of his cock until she shrieked in an orgasm so intense she nearly passed out from the pleasure of it.

When she heard his shout of completion moments later she was still dealing with the aftershocks and wondering how she would survive their next bout.

She yawned, barely noticing when he released the cuffs that bound her to the bed. She cuddled up against him, blindfold still in place, and succumbed to sleep curled up on his chest.

Leo pulled the butt plug out of her ass with a small wince. When she'd threatened to go to someone else to learn, he'd lost it, taking her like an animal when she deserved so much more, so much better, for a wedding night.

Still, from the small smile on her face as she slept in his arms, maybe it wasn't a total fuck-up.

Perhaps he shouldn't have switched the peach plug for the black. It might have been a bit much, especially for a novice.

Still, if this was how his kitten made love when she had very little experience, he couldn't wait to find out how she'd make love a hundred years from now. Or two hundred.

He reached down and pulled up the comforter, trying his best not to disturb her any more than he had to, and settled in to watch her sleep, guilt and bone-deep satisfaction a strange mix in his blood. He'd clean up the toys later. Cuddling his wife was definitely higher on his to-do list.

Chapter Eight

Ruby woke to sunshine and a wary expression on Leo's handsome face. "Good morning," she mumbled.

"Afternoon, actually," he rumbled, his expression wry. "Hungry?"

"Um. I could eat a horse." Ruby stretched that full body stretch that usually made his eyes bug out of his head.

This time, he averted his gaze. "I'll go get some sandwiches." He slid out of bed and reached for his pants.

"Leo? What's wrong?" Ruby frowned.

"Nothing."

"Gee, when I said nothing like that I got the third degree. What should I give you?"

Leo sighed and rubbed the bridge of his nose wearily. "I'm sorry."

"For what?" Ruby had no clue what had him riding the guilt train but was determined to find out.

"I didn't mean to be so…rough…with you earlier. I'm sorry."

She thought about that for a moment watching him pull on his T-shirt. He made his way to the bedroom door and she knew she had to say something now or forever hold her peace. "I never said stop."

He paused, one hand on the doorknob, his back tensing as

he heard the thoughtful note in her voice.

"Think about it, Leo. I never said stop. You said you would if I said it, remember?"

She watched as he turned to her, relief and regret equally mingled. "I lost my head."

"I know."

"I could have hurt you."

"Nope."

He frowned. "What do you mean, nope?"

"I mean, you'd never hurt me."

"Not deliberately! Accidentally!" Leo's hands pushed through his hair, pulling slightly at it. "I lost control, Ruby. I could have hurt you."

She shook her head, coming out of the bed and padding quietly over to him. "Nope." She hooked her arms around his waist and leaned into him, letting him feel her trust in him. The love she was beginning to feel for him warmed her as she cuddled against him, uncaring that she was completely naked.

His arms went around her, hard and secure. "I was scared to death when you didn't wake up after the Binding. That wasn't how I planned on spending our wedding day, Ruby. And then when you did wake up I lost control. I'm so sorry, kitten."

Ruby tensed at the words "wedding day". "Leo?"

"Hmm?" He'd buried his face in her hair and was breathing deep, his big body relaxing into hers.

"When did we get married?"

She felt him stiffen in her arms, and not in the good way. "I explained the bonding to you, remember?"

"Yes, I think so."

"The Claiming, the Vow and the Binding?"

141

"I remember the Claiming, Leo. Details on the rest, please! When did we complete the ceremony, and where was I?"

He stared at her, his expression shocked. "In the front yard. Malmayne tried to take you away from me." Hazy memories began to surface, of Cullen yanking her out of Leo's arms, calling her human with such derision she'd felt soiled. No wonder her harmless teasing had unleashed his beast! "I used earth magic to get him away from you and spoke the Vow." More memories surfaced, of Leo surrounded by incredible power, living tendrils of light that swept all before him as he made his way to her side. "Once the Vow was spoken the Binding took place." He showed her the picture in her mind, of his power spearing into her as he finished the Vow, causing her to black out. "Our truebond is complete now."

She glared at him, her mind whirling a mile a minute. "Don't I have to repeat the Vow for it to be binding?" No pun intended.

His face went still. "It's different with non-Sidhe." She saw the wince more in his eyes than on his face when she raised her brows. "Non-Sidhe don't have to repeat the Vows back for them to work."

She tilted her head, confused. In the kitchen his father *had* repeated the vows. "Didn't Sean repeat them when Aileen said them to him?"

Leo coughed. "Well, no, actually. He didn't. Not the first time, anyway."

Her eyes went wide. "You mean she bound Sean against his will?" She couldn't begin to imagine trying to force Sean to do something he didn't want to do.

Leo chuckled. "Now, that's a story." Leo put his arm around her shoulders, guided her back to the bed, and sat her down on the edge. He moved the chair over by the bed and settled into it directly across from her. "When Mom was sent to Paris to meet with Duncan Malmayne for the first time, it seems Dad was there slumming."

"Slumming?"

"It was the eighteen eighties, and Paris was the place to be at the time. That, or New York, from what I've been told, and Dad had decided to do the European tour thing. Anyway, Mom met Duncan and was agreeable to the marriage contract. Then, one night at the opera, she saw Dad. Said something about their eyes met, he winked at her, and she was lost. She went looking for him the next day."

"The Malmaynes must have been furious."

"They didn't know. Mom snuck out, started asking questions about the blue-eyed Irishman. When she found him she took one whiff of his scent and almost bound him on the spot."

"Wow. Really? What did he smell like?"

Leo smiled. "Mom always says Dad smells like home."

Ruby sighed mistily. "I *really* like your parents."

"Well, it took a few days, and a lot of flirting, but Mom finally got him to kiss her."

"The Tasting."

"Yup. Dad, being a Leprechaun, figured out pretty early that she was Sidhe, but had no idea whether or not she was high-ranking, or even which Court she belonged to."

Ruby shook her head. "Court? You mean like Seelie and Unseelie?"

He looked surprised, and pleased. "Something like that. The Malmaynes and the Jolouns were both White Court and owed allegiance to Glorianna."

"I thought Oberon and Tita—"

His fingers pressed against her lips. "We don't say that name."

She frowned. "Why not?"

"It's said if you say the name of the Dark Queen she'll hear you. Possibly take an interest in you." He shuddered. "You really don't want that."

This just kept getting better and better. "The Dark Queen?"

"The Dark Queen rules the Black Court. It's a long story, but basically the Dark Queen was jealous of the power Oberon had. He was High King over all the fae, and they say he was truly smitten with his queen to the point that he'd bonded with her the same way I've bonded with you. His queen, however, wasn't as smitten. It's said she sold her soul to some dark beings who granted her certain powers. In exchange she was to take over the Court and pay the dark beings in power and blood. She betrayed Oberon, creating the first vampires, tainted creatures created from both humans and other fae, and started a war that almost destroyed us. Somehow Oberon managed to break the truebond they'd shared and shattered the Court."

"I thought a bond couldn't be broken."

"He's the only one I've ever heard of who has managed the feat. No one knows how he did it, but I bet the Hob had a huge hand in it. Now we have the White Court, ruled by Glorianna, the Black Court, ruled by Oberon's ex, and the Gray Court, or Oberon's court. Oberon is still the High King and holds sway over the others, but for the most part he tries not to interfere."

She decided to ignore the fact that a truebond could be broken. She was strangely reluctant to even think about it. "Which court does your family belong to?"

"The Dunnes are White Court, but my family isn't very high up. Shane and I are only lords due to our Joloun blood. Dad's always talked about becoming Gray Court and finally leaving all of the politicking between the families behind, but we've never actually done it."

"Which reminds me. How did your mom get your dad to bond with her?"

"He got tipsy one night and kissed her, and she knew he was the one. Mom made sure he had a bit more wine and managed to get herself into his bed, not that he fought all that hard."

"That sounds familiar." Leo looked completely unrepentant. "Did she take the Vow then?"

"Actually, no. She decided to introduce him to her father first. Needless to say Papa Joloun was not amused, and threatened to have my father 'taken care of'."

"And *then* she spoke the Vow?"

"Nope. Dad left Paris that night. He'd decided she'd be better off with the Malmaynes than with him. Remember, both the Jolouns and Malmaynes were considered Fae of power. Going up against them was no small thing. Add in the fact that he had no clue that Mom had begun to truebond with him, and it just made sense to do what he thought was right. Mom, of course, was heartbroken and refused to go through with the marriage contract. When Papa Joloun locked her in her room and set a few brownie guards, Dad got wind of it."

"How? I mean, if he wasn't in Paris how did he find out?"

"Brownies are also earth spirits, and one of the guards was a personal friend of Dad's and got a message to him. When he found out what was happening to Mom he returned to Paris. By the time he got there he said she no longer looked like the naïve teenage girl he'd first met. She actually had gray in her hair. With the help of the brownies he broke her out of the Joloun mansion and spirited her away. When Duncan Malmayne caught up to them Mom was in the process of binding Dad to her, over his rather loud objections I might add."

"Why did he object? He loved her, right?"

"That's why. He thought he wasn't good enough for her. Anyway, Duncan, realizing it was a truebond, wished them well, but the rest of the families were outraged. Mom and Dad have nothing against Duncan personally, but the rest of the Malmaynes and Jolouns have made it clear they feel that Mom and Dad are beyond the pale."

Ruby's head was swimming with information. "But your parents exchanged Vows downstairs."

"It's customary at the bonding of a Sidhe to a non-Sidhe for the Vows to be exchanged, but that's part of the formal ceremony, not the Binding itself."

"Oh. Sort of a Sidhe wedding, then?"

Leo kissed the back of her hand. "Would you like to do that, Ruby? Have a full ceremony, with friends and family present, and a long white gown? I'm more than willing to do that, kitten, if it makes you happy."

Ruby snapped her mouth closed when Leo chuckled. "Is that a proposal?"

"We're already married, sweetheart, but if you want the formal proposal I can do that."

Ruby bit her lip. "I need time to think, Leo." She reached up and smoothed the frown lines on his brow. "I'm not going to run. Didn't I promise I wouldn't leave you? I just need to think things through, digest everything you've told me. Leo, think about it. It's been a hell of a week."

"I love you, Ruby."

She battled back the tears that started up. His face was totally serious, his eyes sincere and loving despite the hardness of his face. She wasn't certain she could speak past the sudden lump in her throat. "Leo..."

"Shhh." He placed one finger over her lips, his smile lopsided. "You don't have to say it back, not yet."

"Shut the hell up." She felt one of the tears slip past but didn't care. "You big goob." Rising, she turned and settled into his lap, cuddling up to him as his arms went around her. "I want us both to wear rings, you hear me?"

"I hear you, kitten." She felt his sigh of relief as he rested his chin on the top of her head.

"And if you cheat on me I'm cutting off your balls and pickling them."

His involuntary twitch made her giggle. "Duly noted."

"Leo?"

"Yeah?"

"I love you too. How the hell did it happen so fast?"

"Does it matter how fast it happened? To me all that matters is that you do." Leo took her left hand in his and held it out in front of them. Gold sparkles coalesced around their ring fingers until two plain wedding bands appeared. "What design should we make?"

Ruby looked up into his glowing, otherworldly eyes and bit her lip, trying not to laugh. "Horseshoes?"

"Oh, hell." Leo's head thumped the back of the chair as the sparkles dissipated.

"With a blue diamond?"

He closed his eyes on a groan. "*Ruby.*"

"Well, I think ruby balloons would be a bit much, but if that's what you want..."

He cut her off with a kiss that curled her toes. "I was thinking Celtic knot-work myself."

"What, not even a green clover?"

Leo nipped her throat. "Look at our hands," he growled.

Looking down, Ruby gasped. Intricate knot-work rings of white gold sprinkled with white diamonds graced both of their fingers.

"The Celtic knot symbolizes eternity, as does the ring itself."

"So do the diamonds." She blinked tears from her eyes as she stared at the beautiful rings his imagination had wrought. "Diamonds are forever."

"You like them?"

Ruby looked up into Leo's shining eyes and felt her heart turn over. "Oh, yes. I like them. But, there's one other ring I'd like made."

"Which one would that be? Your engagement ring?"

Ruby shook her head. "Read my fantasy, your lordship."

And Leo's face filled with tenderness as a second ring landed on his hand. This one was yellow gold, with an oval shaped black stone. The initials *RH* were carved into the surface of the stone.

Ruby was hardly surprised when she felt the weight of his collar around her neck. Their lips touched, brushed against each other lovingly.

"Mine."

And ever after, neither was quite certain which one of them said it first.

Leo and Ruby dragged themselves to dinner, both drained and ravenous, a sketch of the wedding bands, ring, and collar in Leo's hand. He wanted to talk to his father about finding an earth sprite to do the work for them.

Dinner that evening was both a pleasure and a pain, his family adjusting to his mating and welcoming Ruby with open arms. Always present, however, was the spirit of the missing Shane, and more than once Leo had to pull back his own happiness and deal with the pain and loss they were all still experiencing. Moira tried her best to lighten the mood with her wisecracks, but wasn't able to get more than a half-hearted smile from his mother, and none at all from his father.

"Well, now, don't you all look gloomy," a light tenor voice spoke from the doorway. Turning, Ruby saw a strange man standing in the early twilight, his long red hair bound back with a leather tie, his deep blue eyes gleaming with merriment. He was dressed in black velvet pants and a white poet's shirt, with black leather boots on his feet. He leaned nonchalantly against the doorjamb watching the Dunne family finish their dinner.

Ruby waved hello to the newcomer. "Hi. Are you a friend of the family?"

She felt Leo tense next to her and wondered what she'd done wrong. The man had come in and was obviously at home here. Wasn't he a friend?

The man smiled at her sweetly. "Aye, I am. And you'd be the lovely Ruby, I presume?"

Ruby nodded and watched the red-haired man saunter around the table. In his odd getup, with his long red hair, she'd thought him effeminate. Until he moved. He didn't walk, he *prowled*, his movements sleek and powerful. He reminded her of a jungle cat.

He reached for her hand, placing a delicate kiss on her knuckles. She noticed that his nails had been painted black. "Charmed, my dear, and congratulations on your mating." Laughing blue eyes moved to Leo as the man held her hand.

"Brightest blessings on your mating, Leo! And congratulations on defeating the Malmaynes!"

"We haven't defeated the Malmaynes. They still have Shane." Leo's eyes never left the red-haired man's, and Ruby could have sworn she saw fear in them.

"I'm sorry, we haven't been introduced. You are…?"

"My apologies, my dear. You may call me Robin."

"Robin?"

"Yes. Robin. Robin Goodfellow, actually." His expression was pure mischief, his bluer than blue eyes twinkling at her as he waited for her response.

Ruby blinked.

"Dear gods, don't say it, Ruby."

She ignored Leo's whispered command as her lip began to twitch. "Um. I see Shakespeare was wrong. What's knurly-limbed mean, anyway?"

Robin's eyes widened for a moment, the twinkle in them deepening. "Want to find out?"

"If it has the same results as liposuction? Maybe."

Robin's lips twitched. "Hardly."

"Oh. Well, then." Ruby sighed, the twinkle in her eyes matching Robin's. "So, have you been friends with Leo for long?"

One red brow rose as she waved him to a chair. Without thinking, Ruby got up and poured him and Leo a cup of coffee. "Not for long, no." Ruby noticed his voice was thoughtful as she handed him the cup. He nodded his thanks in a curiously formal gesture.

"Oh, well, we're planning on formalizing our binding with a ceremony once the problem with the Malmaynes is resolved. You'll come, right?"

She ignored Leo's choking and the Dunne's silence as she waited for Robin's answer.

His eyes dancing with unholy amusement, Robin replied, "I wouldn't miss it for the world."

"I like your bondmate." Leo headed out onto the front porch, the Hob following closely behind. "Few there are that aren't terrified of me."

Leo turned his head long enough to see Robin's face. Though his expression was relaxed, Robin's eyes were serious. "You're welcome to come."

Robin's gaze sharpened, softening when he realized Leo meant it. "My thanks, Dunne." Wicked merriment filled the Hob's face. "I'm sure I'll be able to come up with a suitable wedding present."

Leo groaned.

"But that isn't why I came." Robin perched on the railing, balancing on the balls of his feet as he crouched, his head cocked to the side as he stared at Leo. "First, the Malmaynes are not taking your truebond lightly. I fear they may make a move against your Ruby."

Leo's eyes glowed green, his glamour forgotten. "I see. I'll take care of that. And the other?"

Robin looked delighted. "Rumor has it that the Malmayne's caged bird has flown, but where he's flown to is a mystery."

"Shane's free?" Leo couldn't quite believe it, but if the Hob said it was so then he'd have to.

"Aye, which is why I believe they will make a move on your woman. They will need new leverage to get you to agree to their terms." Robin looked down at his black nails. "So, what did you think of Kaitlynn and Cullen?"

151

Leo sighed. "Cullen is indulging Kaitlynn in this, I think. He would be willing, if not happy, to have Shane or Moira fulfill the contract, but Kaitlynn seems fixed on me."

"It's that pretty face of yours. She covets it."

"She can't have it." Leo stared out at the night sky. "Why did you agree to help us?"

Robin chuckled, the first genuine expression Leo had seen on that pretty face. "I owed your mother a favor for something she's not even certain she did." Robin looked up at Leo, his eyes glowing green. "The Hob always pays his debts. Always."

And with that, quick as he'd come, the Hob was gone, his voice floating back on the evening breeze. "Remember: there is another Malmayne."

Jaden blinked, feeling totally put upon. *Where the fuck are you, Duncan?* "You want me to what?"

Kaitlynn sighed, totally exasperated. "Bring me the little human whore, stuff her in the cage Shane was in, and leave her to me. Even someone of your limited intellect can understand that order, yes?"

Jaden snarled. "Careful, sweet cheeks."

He shuddered once again when she smiled. There was just something...off...about her that made him think of spiders.

Jaden hated spiders.

"Bring me the girl, stuff her in a cage, and forget about her. Understand, Mr. Blackthorn?"

Jaden took a deep breath. He did *not* like the direction her thoughts, obvious on her face, were going. "Duncan will not be happy if we hurt an innocent girl."

That saccharine sweet expression crossed her face once

again, and Jaden wondered where Daddy Dearest had gotten to. Cullen was one of the few people capable of dealing with the Deranged Darling. "Duncan can go to hell. Do what I told you, vampire."

Jaden did his best to mimic her smile. "No."

He was pretty sure the slap she landed on his face was supposed to hurt. It probably would have left a bruise on a Sidhe face. On a vampire, it was barely noticeable. "Do as I tell you or I call Mr. West."

The fact that the threat was delivered in the same sickly sweet tones she normally spoke in only made her seem creepier. Time was running out on Kaitlynn Malmayne.

If it wasn't for Duncan, the bitch would already be dead. It was becoming his damn mantra. *If it wasn't for Duncan, if it wasn't for Duncan...*

Jaden turned and stormed out of her office and out of the house. He headed straight towards his car, a classic black Mustang. As soon as he was off Malmayne land he pulled out his cell phone.

"Duncan? Jaden. Where the hell are you? Get your ass to Nebraska. We have more trouble."

He was worried. Duncan hadn't responded mentally in almost a week. Wherever he was, he was out of range of their bond *and* a cell phone tower.

Or he was dead. In which case Jaden had every intention of finding the person or persons responsible and making them pay in exquisitely painful ways.

"Contact Duncan? But why?" Aileen's voice was tight with anxiety and hope.

"I don't know, but Robin mentioned it just before he left. He said, and I quote, 'There is another Malmayne.'"

Ruby watched Leo pace back and forth before the sofa. His parents sat together on it, Sean's hand resting firmly on top of Aileen's clasped ones. Ruby had the impression he was keeping her from wringing her fingers to pieces. Moira was currently reading in her room. Ruby knew that the pressure of Leo's mating and Shane's continued absence was beginning to tell on her.

"Maybe he meant Duncan and Moira could fulfill the contract." Ruby turned back to Leo to catch his reaction.

"Oh, no! Duncan's *much* too old for Moira!" Aileen's voice was very firm.

"Um, no offense, but you guys live practically forever. What would age have to do with it?"

"Moira's barely fifty years old!"

Leo nodded. "Anyone under fifty is considered a child still."

"What does that make you? A precocious teenager?"

Leo's expression heated. "Yup. Wait until I hit my prime."

"Oh, hell." Ruby rolled her eyes. "So how old is Duncan?"

"Duncan Malmayne is over five hundred years old."

Ruby whistled. "Wow. A mature man, huh?" She ignored Leo's growl and focused on Aileen. "So he'd have to wait to claim her?"

Aileen looked absolutely horrified. "My Moira couldn't handle a man like Duncan Malmayne!"

Ruby smiled tightly. "Moira could handle just about anything." She still hadn't quite forgiven Moira for the pain she'd caused Leo, despite the fact that they'd apparently made up. She turned to Sean. "Do leprechauns mature more quickly than Sidhe?"

Sean nodded reluctantly. "Yes. By fifty we're considered

Dare to Believe

adults, but our life spans are shorter than the Sidhe."

Ruby looked at Aileen, who had "stubborn refusal" written all over her face. She shrugged. "It was just a thought."

"Perhaps he meant Duncan could help us get Kaitlynn off my back." Leo ran both hands through his hair, tugging on it in frustration. "I just wish Shane was back already."

"Can we take the Hob's word for it that Shane is free?" Sean's voice and expression were skeptical.

Leo nodded. "Yeah, Robin still feels he owes Mom for something, so I believe him. Besides," Leo shot an irritated look at Ruby, "he likes my wife."

Ruby grinned. "Your wife likes him, too." And despite their conversation that one word sent a thrill through her. She was married to Leo Dunne.

Granted, in the human world it wasn't legal, but they'd be taking care of that once Shane was home.

Leo tried to stare her down, one black brow rising arrogantly. "Don't like him too much."

She blew him a kiss just as Sean bolted up from the sofa.

"Sean?" Aileen's face was full of fear as she stared at her husband.

"I feel Shane!"

Ruby got to see just how quickly a leprechaun could move on his land. Sean disappeared so quickly she didn't even see a blur.

Leo said something to his mother in that lyrical language Ruby didn't know then ran out the door after his father at a much more human pace. Aileen and Ruby stared at each other, Aileen's eyes filled with hope and dread.

"What's happening?" Moira's voice came from the top of the stairs. She made her way down, a light frown on her face. "I just saw Dad run like a bat out of hell down the drive, with Leo right behind him."

"Shane." Aileen beamed at her daughter, tears in her eyes. "Your father sensed Shane."

Moira gasped, her hand clenching on the banister. "He's sure?"

At Aileen's nod, Moira let out a war-whoop that practically shook the house. "Where is he?"

"Right behind me, darling."

Jaden watched the human, Ruby, turn to face him. He was leaning against the doorjamb, making sure to keep his body out of the Dunne house. Some vampires really *did* have to be invited inside, and he was hoping this would lull the women into a false sense of security.

"Shane?" Ruby tried to peer around him, her expression happy. He hated that very soon he'd be forced to wipe that expression from her face.

"Shane's not there," Aileen answered. She stepped forward, her Sidhe power wrapped around her like a golden cloak. "Get away from my house, vampire." Aileen began to glow. The golden flecks sprinkling her skin held a life of their own as they danced in a hypnotic pattern, one that Jaden ignored. He smirked at Aileen, keeping it smug even though he felt anything but.

"Of course." His gaze drifted over to Ruby. "As soon as the girl comes out." His eyes changed, black growing impossibly blacker, pulling his prey to him. "Come here, girl."

His voice was seduction itself, a promise that coiled around the woman's senses and tightened, drawing her forward one hesitant step at a time.

"I don't think so, vampire."

He blinked at the vision of redheaded fury standing between him and his prey. Moira Dunne growled, positioning herself in front of Ruby, ready to defend her sister-in-law to the death.

Jaden tsk'd. It wouldn't do to let Moira know he was impressed. It took a lot of guts for a Sidhe that young to stand up to a fully mature vampire, no matter the circumstances. "Get out of the way, sweetheart. I'm not here for you."

"Are you kidding me? Do you know what my brother would do if I let someone like you touch his mate? Hell, he'll probably be pissed you breathed the same air."

Jaden didn't bother to hide his fangs as they dropped down. "Sidhe. So stuck up." He focused his will on Moira and pulled. "Come out here, my pretty. Come to me, sweet." His gaze remained locked on her face though it longed to roam over her luscious curves. "I've always been partial to redheads."

Moira began to move forward. He heard a gasp of fear.

"No!" Aileen pushed Ruby out of the way in a desperate attempt to get to her daughter, causing Ruby to stumble. Moira turned and, without blinking, backhanded her mother into the wall.

Huh. Wonder what that's all about. Apparently Moira had some unresolved issues with her mother. He didn't bother hiding his grin. Aileen had already made her opinion of him known.

Aileen slumped to the ground, dazed, as Moira continued forward.

"I thought you preferred brunettes?" Ruby asked, obviously trying to get his attention off Moira.

Jaden kept his eyes on what he suspected was the *real*

prize in the Dunne house. "Sorry, sweet. I've always had a thing for feisty redheads." Moira started to step over the threshold and into the vampire's waiting arms.

"Oh, hell." Ruby ran forward, pushing in front of Moira. "Leave her alone, Bunnicula, I'm here."

Jaden blinked, accidentally breaking his thrall on Moira. "Bunnicula? *Bunnicula?* Do I look like the type to suck on carrots?"

Moira shuddered and stepped back. "I don't know. Bunnicula seems pretty appropriate. How many carrots *have* you sucked on?" And she smirked in that annoying way that men everywhere recognized.

"Women." Jaden shook his head sadly. "They don't pay me enough for this shit." He glared at Ruby. "Come on out here and let's get this over with."

"No." Moira pulled Ruby back, once again standing in front of her.

Jaden sighed. *Damn. Now I'm going to have to bruise that porcelain skin.* "You know, I tried to do this nicely. Now I'm just going to have to do it the other way." And with that, he stepped over the threshold, his eyes once again glowing red.

"Um, I thought he couldn't come in here without an invitation." Ruby backed up warily.

"Wrong kind of vampire, apparently," Moira breathed, backing up along with her.

"Apparently." Jaden crooked a finger at Ruby, allowing the nail to grow into a long, black claw. He had no intention of actually *using* his claws on either girl, but damn if they weren't great for intimidation. He only hoped they worked. "Come here, girl. Someone wants to see you."

"No!" And Moira rushed him, determination in every line of

Dare to Believe

her small body.

Moira knew some kick boxing from the way she used her feet. Jaden was beyond impressed. She lashed out with a spinning heel kick that would have knocked the head off a lesser being, one not meant to be a soldier in the Dark Queen's army.

Fortunately, thanks to his son-of-a-bitch sire, her ploy didn't work. All it did was rock his head on his neck. He moved to block her next strike, holding his greater strength in check. It had to be obvious to Moira that she was going to lose. He could see it in her face that she knew she couldn't defeat him, but that rock solid determination to keep him away from her sister-in-law still burned brightly enough to *really* impress him.

Out of the corner of his eye he saw Ruby dash out of the house, screaming for lover-boy at the top of her lungs.

Perfect.

Time to end this. Jaden put Moira down as gently as he could, knocking her out with the least amount of damage he could inflict.

He stared down at Moira with a wicked smile. "Beautiful, brave Moira." He brushed his hands through her hair, reluctant to leave her behind.

She'd proven herself to him. Now he was going to prove himself to her.

He pressed a soft kiss to her lips just before he sank his teeth into her neck.

That kiss promised that they weren't done. Not by a long shot.

"You shouldn't have interfered, beautiful." He stroked her hair away from her forehead, his expression hot and possessive. He licked her sweet *leprechaun* blood from his lips. He'd forgotten that about her, though he'd never forget it again. He pressed a soft kiss to her unresponsive lips. "I'll be seeing you soon."

"Leo! Leo! Help me!" Ruby ran screaming, knowing somehow that hiding wouldn't work against the creature that pursued her.

Ruby felt a strong wind pass her by and she stopped, hoping against hope that Sean was heading back to the house.

The roar that came from the Dunne house had the hair on the back of her neck standing on end. The ground beneath her feet buckled and heaved. Sean was letting loose his anger in a very visible way. Ruby gasped out a sob and turned back towards the house, every fiber of her being calling out for her mate.

"Ruby?" She turned, nearly falling. Leo's arms came around her, protecting her. "Shhh. It's okay, kitten, I have you."

"There's a vampire in the house with your mother and sister," she gasped out, falling against him and hugging him to her so tightly she was surprised his ribs didn't crack.

She felt him stiffen. "Vampire? In Dad's house?"

She nodded, still gasping for breath. Running was so not her forte. "Uh-huh. Moira fought him."

"Holy hell." And Leo took off running towards the house.

Leaving her alone on the dark driveway, half a mile from the house. "Oh no."

A dark figure stepped onto the driveway, its eyes glowing an eerie red. "Hello, beautiful." The vampire sighed, his voice pulling her into his arms.

"Ruby!" Leo ran back down the drive, horrified. His mate

was in a strange car, being driven away. Being taken from him. The ground at his feet rippled with his anger. If he'd been faster, he could have stopped the vampire. But this wasn't his land, and what little leprechaun blood that did run through his veins wasn't enough to save her. Leo gritted his teeth, knowing his own stupidity in leaving her in the driveway had led to her abduction. He began running back towards the house and his car, his only thought to get to his wife.

The vampire would pay for taking what was his.

Jaden looked at the woman sleeping next to him and grimaced. Leo was going to take his head off his shoulders for drugging his bondmate, but it was the only way he could think of to get the woman to Kaitlynn without hurting her. Her mind was fairly strong. Getting her to walk calmly off Dunne land, without alerting Sean Dunne to his presence, had taken most of his strength. He'd had just enough left to get her to swallow the roofie he'd brought with him before seating her in the car and taking off.

Thank the gods he'd had a taste of sexy leprechaun before leaving the ole homestead, or he would never have pulled it off.

Damn, but Moira made him hot. Just picturing her lips in that maddening sneer gave him a hell of a hard-on. Add that glorious red-gold hair, that pale, smooth complexion, and blue eyes a man could drown in, and you had one happy, horny vampire. She fought like a she-cat to defend her sister-in-law and mother, something Jaden could admire even as he deplored the need for it.

Damn Kaitlynn for making him meet a woman like that under circumstances like these. He wished he could tell her he was on her side, but he couldn't.

Not yet.

He could feel, through the light blood bond he'd established, that Moira was well. He could feel her irritation at being fussed over, her fear of what he'd do to Ruby, and did his best to send his reassurances down the light link he'd established with his bite. He'd keep Ruby safe, if only because she meant something to the feisty redhead.

If Duncan didn't come back soon Jaden was going to kill Kaitlynn personally and damn the consequences. Either way, he had every intention of coming back to Dunne land and finishing what he'd started with their daughter.

With a grin, Jaden wondered how Duncan would react to his blood-bonding the leprechaun. He couldn't wait to find out.

He had the feeling the two of them were going to like each other.

By the time Leo made it back to the house, Shane had arrived. The vampire had told the truth about that, at least. Once they had a weary, battered Moira and an equally weary Shane settled in the kitchen, the vampire was well away from the farm. But at least Leo now knew where the vampire had more than likely taken his wife.

Leo, his eyes filled with equal measures of fury and fear, dialed the number his mother handed him.

"Duncan Malmayne? My name is Leo Dunne. I'm going to kill your sister." Leo quietly shut the phone, ignoring his mother's gasp. He turned on his heel and headed towards his car.

Kaitlynn Malmayne had gone too far, and now she was going to die.

Chapter Nine

Using the directions Shane had provided, Leo made his way into Omaha. His blood was boiling with fury and guilt despite Moira's weird assurances that somehow she knew Ruby was currently safe. When Leo asked her how she could be so sure, she'd blushed and refused to answer.

Something else the damn vampire would have to answer for. The wounds on his sister's neck had healed quickly, but the fucking vamp had left a hickey.

Leo knew from his brother's description that the Malmaynes had kept him on a plush property just outside the Omaha city limits. Apparently, they'd bought the property some time in the nineties and built a house with over twelve thousand square feet of living space on around twenty acres, most of which was heavily wooded. The only areas not wooded were the pool area and the formal garden the Malmaynes had insisted be put in and maintained.

Shane had also said the house, while structurally quite beautiful, lacked a soul.

Leo pulled the Navigator to the side of the road about a mile from the Malmayne's mansion. Getting out, he grabbed his flashlight, pulled on a leather glove and took hold of Shane's tire iron. Jogging into the night, he counted on his own magic to get him in the front door.

If even one hair on Ruby's head was hurt, the vampire wouldn't be the only one Leo went after with the tire iron.

Ruby opened her eyes to a white, sterile room. She tried to lift her head, but found she couldn't. It felt like it weighed a ton. She could barely turn her head, but when she succeeded the wave of dizziness and nausea made her glad she hadn't been able to lift it. She stared at the large mirror that graced one wall and barely restrained the urge to roll her eyes.

"I've either been abducted by aliens or the Feds." Her speech was slurred. She vaguely remembered swallowing a pill a handsome, dark-haired man handed to her, but everything else was a blank.

A male voice chuckled softly from behind her. "How are you feeling?"

"Dizzy, weak, pissed off. You?"

The voice chuckled again, and then replied, "Fine, thanks."

"Oh. Glad to hear it. Not."

The vampire sighed and stepped into view. "I don't have a great deal of time, so listen well, Ruby. Kaitlynn's insane."

"Oh. Really?" Ruby licked her lips. It tasted like something had crawled into her mouth and died there some time ago. "Didn't notice."

"Hard to miss, actually. I'm going to drug you again."

Ruby couldn't quite hide her wince. "Why?"

"She can't get inside your head if you're drugged out of it."

She thought about that briefly, about what an insane Sidhe could force her to do in her own mind. Her little dance with Cullen backed up the vampire's words. "Drugs are good."

The vampire smiled. "Thought you'd see it my way. Open wide, sweetheart."

Ruby opened her mouth and allowed him to place the pill on her tongue. When he gave her a drink of water to swallow it down, she nearly choked.

"Careful."

"Why are you helping me now?"

The vampire threw a quick glance at the door, and then leaned down over her body. With a start she realized that he really was incredibly handsome, something she hadn't had a chance to notice before. "Kaitlynn is a bitch. I work for Duncan, but he's gone missing. Kaitlynn decided to appropriate my services in her brother's absence, and holds something over my head to force my compliance. However, I don't like what she's doing here, so I'm going to do my best to stop her at every turn without getting myself killed in the process. Simple enough?"

"Did you help Shane escape?"

He nodded happily. "I knew you were a smart girl."

Ruby blinked sleepily and yawned, her head beginning to spin. "Did you hurt Moira?"

His cheerful façade dropped away immediately. In its place was a ruthless predator. "The only people who are completely safe from me are Duncan Malmayne and Moira Dunne."

"Kaitlynn might hurt her, to get to Leo." Her speech was barely human. The medication began to take effect, making it nearly impossible to keep her eyes open.

Red flames danced in his eyes. "No. She won't. I'll kill her first." Ruby felt a cool hand smooth her hair down as she drifted into unconsciousness. The last thing she heard was the vampire's departure as he left the cell she lay in.

Jaden stood outside Ruby's cell, watching her sleep. Duncan hadn't contacted him yet; soon, he'd have no choice but to remove Kaitlynn permanently. He couldn't risk Moira's life, or Ruby's, on the whim of the madwoman his bond-brother called sister.

Ruby slept peacefully, her heart rate normal, her blood flowing smoothly through her veins. Moira lay awake somewhere in her house, scared for her sister-in-law and...brother? *Ah, Leo is on his way.*

Surprise, surprise. He wondered how close the Sidhe was to the Malmayne estate. He did his best to send his feisty little blonde reassurances, but until he deepened the bond between them fleeting impressions was all he could send her.

He tried to convey through their bond that Ruby slept peacefully. Unfortunately, not knowing where Leo was, he couldn't help her there.

It was with real pleasure he felt his little leprechaun relax a little.

For that small amount of implied trust, he would ensure Ruby's life with his own. For the first time in over a century, someone other than Duncan had a hold on his cynical heart.

Kaitlynn stepped into the room and he watched out of the corner of his eye, curious to see her reaction. She glided over to the one-way glass, her eyes glued to the sleeping figure of Ruby Dunne.

"When will she wake up?"

The sick anticipation in her voice made him shudder. "I don't know."

Kaitlynn took a step closer to the glass. "How much did you give her?"

"Only the one."

Her eyes narrowed, her lips pouted, and in that moment her smooth loveliness turned hard and ugly. "Wake her."

Jaden turned to her, one brow lifted in disbelief. "And how would you like me to accomplish that, your highness? Intravenous caffeine?"

Her lips turned up sweetly, but did nothing to dispel the frost in her eyes. "You know, Jaden? Perhaps your usefulness is at an end."

If he hadn't been expecting treachery of some kind the rowan stake might have found its mark. Jaden screamed as the stake entered his back, the pain nearly crippling him. He fell to the floor, slowing his heart rate, nearly stopping his breathing as Kaitlynn laughed in delight.

Jaden closed his eyes and lost his hold on consciousness.

On the Dunne farm, Moira sat up from her bed, screaming in horror. Her back bore an ugly, bloody wound, and none of the family could figure out how it got there.

On a private runway just outside Omaha, a blond man with steel gray eyes gasped, his hand going to his back. When he pulled his hand away, it was covered in blood.

Those steel gray eyes glittered like twin stars as the man dashed towards the car waiting for him at the end of the runway.

"Home. Now. Hurry."

Duncan Malmayne stared out the car window as his driver took off at top speed, his eyes haunted and full of regret as he heard Jaden's brief mental scream.

"*Jaden.* Damn you, Kaitlynn."

Leo knew the moment he stepped onto Malmayne land. Something in it cried out to him, the sound of earth that had been forced to absorb pain, degradation, even murder. The call was faint to his senses, but he knew any full-blooded earth sprite would avoid this place like the plague.

Leo clenched his hands, feeling savagely angry. He had no idea where on the estate Ruby was, but there was one way to find out.

He reached deep down inside himself, to the green pool of peace and tranquility that made up his leprechaun half. Using that energy, Leo extended his essence around the Malmayne property, defining what was *his* to his leprechaun senses. Cautious, he hoped that the earth would accept him.

His father had told him if the earth did take him in it would be the most incredible experience of his life. If it didn't, it would be the most incredibly painful.

He felt a tentative caress, the questioning tendrils entering his mind, finding every nook and cranny, every memory, every experience he'd ever had. It lingered over things that confused him (getting drunk on spiked punch on New Year's when he'd been twelve, throwing up in the bushes) and completely ignored others (most of the women he'd dated didn't even rate a glance). It watched his memories of his family like video clips, fast forwarding then stopping to watch a clip that particularly interested it. It loved images of his father, lingered like a caress over his mother, and especially loved anything to do with Moira. It skipped a number of Shane memories, possibly because it already knew Shane.

When it hit Ruby, it drew back for a moment, and Leo feared he would be rejected. He felt the earth begin to watch as he purposely began playing his memories, from his first scent of vanilla and peaches, wandering the office to find that elusive scent, to finally meeting her. Those memories drew the earth in as he replayed tasting her. How she barely argued over being essentially kidnapped, all because he needed her to be with him. How she'd been curious, and cautious, but not once had she rejected him on any level, and how he cherished her for that. He knew the earth felt their love.

When the earth took back over, Leo eased off. It replayed his memories of how Ruby had been hurt by Cullen, and he felt its anger.

With a start, Leo realized he was starting to feel what the earth felt. Blood and pain were a distant nausea; he knew the vampire was down. Somehow, he also knew the vampire (*"Jaden"*, the earth whispered with affection and regret) had tried his damnedest to help both Ruby and Shane. He saw how Jaden had been partially responsible for Shane's getaway, and felt some remorse for the violent feelings he'd harbored towards the vampire. Like his own private movie show, he saw in fast forward everything Jaden had done, first to help Shane, then to help Ruby, and how the vampire had nearly paid with his life.

With a grin, Leo felt the bond of the leprechaun and his land snap into place like a lover's first caress, shocking, intimate, and incredibly pleasurable.

He knew where everyone on his land was. What everyone on his land was. He knew Jaden was close to death. He knew Kaitlynn was staring at...

Ruby! He could feel the heavy, drugged sleep his bonded slept under, could feel Kaitlynn's rage when they couldn't rouse her. Felt her kick the downed vampire, and knew somehow that Ruby's drugged state had been no part of Kaitlynn's plan for her.

Fine, the vampire lives. Leo used the earth to amplify his Sidhe powers, cloaking his presence from all prying eyes. He began cautiously making his way towards the house. Not being fully leprechaun, he couldn't move with the preternatural speed his father could. However, there were other things being part Sidhe provided. Since he *knew* where each and every person on the estate was, it was child's play to cloak their minds. Any sounds he made were automatically assumed to be something natural to whatever part of the estate they were on. With the very earth itself lending him its power, he found he could tamper with the senses of everyone on the estate, even Kaitlynn, without them feeling it.

He stopped abruptly as a new sense filtered in. The pain and death he'd felt hadn't been Jaden. Jaden was still alive, down below the house.

The death had been Cullen's. His body was buried on the estate, in the formal gardens he'd loved so much. Kaitlynn had poisoned him.

He felt someone new step onto the property.

"Duncan." He could see the older man through the earth, sensed his deep well of power, and knew his rage and grief as if it were his own. Changing his plans, Leo moved to intercept him.

"Malmayne," he whispered in the other man's ear from ten feet away.

The blond man stopped, his expression wary. "Dunne."

"You can't stop me, Malmayne."

"My sister took your wife, Dunne, and nearly killed my bond-brother. I have no intention of stopping you."

Leo was startled. A Sidhe of Duncan Malmayne's prominence would never claim to have a vampire as a bond-brother. The vampire must have done something extraordinary to have Duncan claim him as his own. "Jaden lives. The land is sustaining him."

Duncan's silver eyes widened in shock before carefully

blanking. "You've claimed the land."

Leo noted he didn't sound surprised. "How else could I find my wife safely?"

Duncan nodded. "I will, of course, deed the property over to you as a wedding present."

Leo moved in front of Duncan before removing the cloud from the other man's senses. "Kaitlynn still needs to pay for what was done to my sister, my brother and Ruby."

"Your sister?" Duncan frowned, showing no surprise at Leo sudden appearance before him.

"The vampire... Jaden fought her, knocked her unconscious and fed from her just before he took my mate."

"Ah." Duncan sighed his understanding. "Your sister is fine. If Jaden truly wished to hurt her, she would have died the moment she touched him. If he allowed her to fight him it was because he was protecting her as best he could."

Leo raised a brow. "He has a strange way of protecting her."

"And if your mate had gotten away from him he could have claimed it was because of the fight."

"A lie without lying?" Duncan nodded, confirming Leo's thought. "He's kept Ruby drugged so that Kaitlynn can't mess with her mind."

"I'm not surprised. Despite evidence to the contrary Jaden is a good man." Duncan looked towards the mansion. "Kaitlynn must know we're here by now. We would be on the security cameras."

Leo held up his hand as Duncan started to move towards the house. "I have the senses of every person on this estate clouded except yours, Jaden's and Ruby's. No one knows we're here."

Duncan stared towards the house, a scowl on his face. "I

need to find my father. I need to know why he allowed things to go this far."

Leo sighed. "Your father is no longer alive."

Duncan turned back to him, his eyes icily blank. "Excuse me?"

Leo could no longer see Duncan as the earth fed him information rapidly. "Kaitlynn did something to his after-dinner brandy. Curare, I think, but the earth isn't sure since it didn't come from here." Leo shuddered. Kaitlynn had buried her father before he was completely dead. "She buried him in the formal gardens. The earth still screams of his pain."

The rage and grief coming off Duncan Malmayne increased tenfold. Leo could feel the man's power radiating off him. Silver sparks danced in the air around him. In the coldest voice Leo had ever heard Duncan whispered, "Leave Kaitlynn to me."

"Kaitlynn needs to pay for hurting my mate," Leo growled, his own eyes glowing green.

Duncan smiled, and Leo tried to hide his shiver at the chill in it. "Jaden will be hungry when he wakes up."

"Feeding a vampire is hardly fitting punishment for the crimes your sister has committed."

"I never said she'd survive the feeding." Duncan's head tilted, as if listening to something only he could hear. "Jaden is...displeased with my sister." His expression turned feral. "And he has a very vivid imagination."

Leo moved silently through the front of the house. The few sounds he did make he was able to muffle in the minds of the guards. Duncan was moving around the back of the house, the other Sidhe having decided to use the kitchen entrance. He'd taken out the guards stationed there before heading to intercept

Leo. Whether they were loyal to the Malmaynes in general or Kaitlynn in particular would be sorted out later.

He could feel Ruby beneath him, deep in the earth. She was beginning to wake up. Apparently the stimulants Kaitlynn had ordered administered were beginning to work. He could feel Jaden tensing himself, rousing from the half sleep that had kept his heartbeat slow. If Jaden moved to block Kaitlynn, odds were good he wouldn't survive. The vampire had lost too much blood.

There was another in the room with them, someone the earth found repulsive (*"Jeremy West"*, the earth whispered). Another vampire, he was tall, with dark hair and eyes, cold in a way Jaden wasn't. He ignored most of what Kaitlynn was doing, only smiling when Ruby moaned.

That look on West's face nearly had Leo losing control. The man's eyes glowed red, and his teeth had dropped.

"He hungers."

Leo decided enough was enough. To hell with skulking. It was time to see exactly how well a leprechaun and his land worked together.

Ruby opened her eyes, wondering what in the hell she'd been drinking the night before. There was a horrible taste in her mouth. "Wha' the hell you been feeding me? Road kill?" She moaned.

"Welcome to your new home, human," a feminine, familiar voice said.

Ruby shut her eyes with a groan. "I'm going back to sleep. Wake me when Leo kills you." The sharp slap stung even through the drug haze. "Ow."

"Go back to sleep and I'll cut off your finger and pour a

glass of your blood for the vampire."

Ruby cautiously peeked, not happy to see Kaitlynn smiling sweetly down at her. "You have spinach stuck in your teeth."

The blonde reared back, one hand covering her mouth, her eyes horrified. Ruby snickered.

Kaitlynn removed her hand and stood tall and proud. "Allow me to introduce you to a friend of mine." She waved languidly. A tall, dark-haired man stepped into view. His eyes glowed red and his teeth were pointed. "Jeremy West." She simpered up at the vampire. "Jeremy, meet your dinner."

"Swell." Ruby desperately tried not to tremble at the anticipation she saw in West's face. The vampire was staring down at her like she was coated in melted Godiva and he was a confirmed chocoholic.

West licked his lips. "Mmm. She's going to taste *sweet*."

Ruby found herself fighting a hysterical laugh. "You have a great future in porno movies."

His arm snapped up, ready to strike down at her, and she flinched. There was no expression on his face at all. *Damn. No sense of humor.*

"I wouldn't do that if I were you."

Huh? I thought Ms. Schizo would adore having me battered.

"Too many bruises and I won't get Leo's cooperation."

Oh. That explains that.

"Besides, I'd prefer to hurt her myself."

Everything around her went dark.

Leo watched from the shadows as Duncan signaled his readiness to enter the...*dungeon,* was the only word he could think of to describe it, below the Malmayne estate. He nodded, prepared to move—

The terrified screams ripped into his soul and nearly tore it apart. Gone was any thought of moving silently. He rushed into the room, determined to save Ruby no matter the cost.

She was in some sort of glass and concrete cage. He could see Kaitlynn and Jeremy West standing over her. Her body arched off the slab she was lying on, every muscle straining against invisible shackles. The only breaths she took were to keep screaming.

Kaitlynn smiled, and Leo lost it. The earth trembled beneath his feet. His eyes fell on the electronic lock on the door, and he wondered if he could manipulate it open. It was made of metal, which was of the earth, and was on his land. If that didn't work he would bring the entire house down to save his mate if he had to.

But before he could move, Jaden was there, ripping the door off its hinges and throwing it away, almost hitting Duncan in the process. Leo flew through the opening, barely catching a glimpse of Jaden collapsing to the floor again with a groan.

"I wouldn't come any closer, if I were you."

Leo didn't even hesitate. The power of the earth surged through him. He rushed forward and backhanded Kaitlynn with all his strength, grimly satisfied when he heard a bone crack. She staggered back, stunned and howling in pain.

Ruby's screams abruptly cut off.

"Step back, Sidhe."

He turned to see Ruby held by West. One of West's hands was wrapped around her throat, the other around her waist. Her feet dangled above the floor, her sweat-drenched hair hanging limp around her pale face. She looked terrified.

"I can snap her neck like a twig." The tips of West's fangs poked out to caress his bottom lip obscenely. "Or you can cooperate."

Leo felt the earth tremble again in response to his rage.

"It's simple, really." Kaitlynn caressed her cheek, her expression once again cloyingly sweet. "You take me to mate, and your...Ruby...doesn't get hurt any more than she's already been."

"Choose not to cooperate, and she becomes my lunch."

"That's quite enough, Mr. West." Kaitlynn smoothed out her skirt with shaking hands. "Well, Leo?"

"Do it and you'll never get any again in your entire long existence."

Leo's mouth quirked up at Ruby's growled order. That was all he'd needed to ensure that Kaitlynn's plans were destroyed. He shrugged. "I told you my mate doesn't like to share." He looked over at West. "And neither do I."

He only meant to throw the man off balance, Raising a tiny section of the floor a few feet off the ground would have accomplished that nicely, and hopefully startle the other man into letting go of Ruby.

Instead, a full circular foot of concrete, gravel and dirt pushed upward at an alarming rate, smashing West against the ceiling so fast he had no time to react, or even yell. Ruby screamed. Blood and tissue spurted out of the flattened body of the man who'd been holding her, drenching her in the disgusting fluids. The concrete and dirt circle pushed up until the vampire's arms were severed, dropping a shrieking Ruby to the ground. When she hit the ground he could see that her shirt and jeans had been torn through in spots, revealing a mass of cuts and scraps that would have to be tended to and soon.

"Oh, God. I'm gonna..."

He watched helplessly as Ruby vomited. He was stunned by what he'd done to West. Bits of the vampire were still dripping down the new column of earth.

At least I'm pretty sure the son of a bitch is dead. Too bad his stomach was threatening to join Ruby's in the old heave-ho.

"Wash her off, quickly." Leo turned to find Jaden leaning against the doorjamb, a scowl on his face. "Hurry! *His blood is in those wounds!*"

"Fuck!" He picked up Ruby and sprinted for the stairs, moving faster than he'd ever done before. He had to wash the vampire blood off of her before it was too late.

He was fairly certain his still heaving mate had no desire to become a vampire.

Duncan glided into the dungeon room, beautiful and dangerous. Jaden watched him with bleary eyes, knowing he didn't have long before he collapsed again. It would be worth it, though, to see Duncan give his sister the smack-down she deserved.

"Hello, Kaitlynn."

The Deranged Darling flinched at the sight of her big brother, the livid bruise on her face in stark contrast to the pallor of her skin. "Duncan." Her voice was slurred, no doubt due to the hit Dunne had landed.

Duncan was staring at Kaitlynn in a very scary way. Jaden watched and wondered what the Sidhe was up to. He doubted it would go the way he hoped. The woman *was* Duncan's sister, unfortunately. "Blood debt is owed, and you're going to pay it."

"On whose authority?" One brow tried to rise, but then she winced, the action pulling at her bruised cheek.

"On mine, as Lord of Clan Malmayne." The authority in

Duncan's voice sent shivers down Jaden's spine. He allowed his teeth to drop, determined to back Duncan with his last drop of blood if need be. If his bond-brother was actually going to make Kaitlynn pay for her crimes then Jaden wanted in on the action, even if he only got to be a spectator.

"Father is lord, not you." Her chin rose. She almost managed a sneer, but her broken cheek prevented it.

"Father is dead, buried in the formal gardens." Jaden's jaw dropped. How in hell had he missed *that*? It was damn near impossible to hide death from a vampire.

He glanced at the column that pinned Jeremy West to the ceiling. Perhaps the other vamp had somehow managed to hide the tell-tale signs?

Kaitlynn's skin had gone pale, her expression filled with trepidation.

"Dead by your hand, I believe." Duncan circled his sister, his eyes cold and without mercy. "For your crime of murder, the sentence is death."

Kaitlynn gasped.

Goodbye, bitch. Jaden laughed internally, delighted at this turn of events.

"For the crime of kidnapping and torture: also death."

She whimpered.

"For the crime of the attempted murder of my bondmate: death."

Wait, bondmate? Jaden nearly chortled. Duncan was breaking out a truly archaic definition of the bond they shared, if he was calling Jaden his *bondmate*. By using that term, he increased the level of Kaitlynn's crime from attempted murder to cardinal sin.

"Sentence to be carried out immediately." Duncan turned

to Jaden with a grim look. "She's all yours."

Jaden bowed, as best he could in his wounded state, to the man he'd pledged his allegiance and part of his heart to almost a century ago.

Then he turned to Kaitlynn and smiled sweetly. The pain subsided at his lord's permission to feed.

He was very, *very* hungry.

He let the predator in him surface, using everything he was to ensure the Deranged Darling paid her debt in full.

Not one drop of Kaitlynn's blood tainted the floor. Jaden made sure of it.

"Fuck, fuck, fuck," Leo chanted. He pulled Ruby under the warm water, desperate to get the tainted blood off of her. He didn't bother removing her ruined clothes first, just dunked her under the shower and rinsed her as fast as he could. He completely ignored his own clothes, not caring that he was now soaked along with her. He was pretty sure Duncan could spare them some new ones.

"Leo?"

Her quavering, weepy voice nearly did him in. "It's okay, kitten. I'm here."

She collapsed into his arms, sobbing, and he nearly sobbed with her. He held her and rocked her, making nonsense noises in her ear just to let her know he was there.

He began to sing softly, a lullaby in the Sidhe tongue. Eventually her weeping slowed. When she began ripping her clothes from her body, he didn't question, just helped. And when she picked them up and threw them as hard as she could out the shower door, he helped with that, too.

Finally, her crying stopped completely. She drowsed in his

arms, only the occasional sniffle letting him know she was still awake. He picked her up and carried her into the adjoining bedroom, laying her wet body down on top of the coverlet. He went back into the bathroom and turned off the water. He grabbed a towel and returned to her. He didn't want her out of his sight.

"You're okay, kitten. Nobody's ever going to hurt you again."

He winced as the gentle swipes of the towel against her abraded back drew a hiss of pain from her. When he was done, he rapidly stripped himself down, dried himself off, and slipped between the sheets. He really didn't give a fuck if Duncan was offended or not. Ruby needed to rest, so she was going to rest. He wasn't even sure whose bedroom they were in, other than it wasn't Kaitlynn's. The stench of the other woman would have driven him from the room once Ruby was cleaned off.

Ruby cuddled up against his chest, hiding her face in his shoulder. The occasional shudder still wracked her body.

If I hadn't left her in the driveway none of this would have happened. Guilt ate at him like acid, but he just couldn't deal with that right now. Ruby needed him.

"Show me what she did to you, kitten." He hoped if he could get inside her mind, he'd be able to fix whatever it was Kaitlynn had done to terrify her.

She shook her head. "Nope. Not going there *ever* again."

He nodded. He'd get to see it when she was ready, he was determined on that, but there was no point in traumatizing her further. "Then tell me."

She drew a deep breath. "Have you ever seen those horror movies where someone's strapped down to a table, a bit is put in their mouth, some weird contraption is strapped to their head, and then someone else throws the switch?"

Leo stiffened. "Electrocution?"

Ruby nodded, never moving her face from his shoulder.

Oh, the bitch died way too easy. He'd felt Kaitlynn's death while they'd been in the shower, but he'd been too focused on Ruby to pay it much attention. He was going to ask Duncan and Jaden to bury her body somewhere far, far away, where her evil would no longer poison his land.

He felt Ruby moving against him and looked down. She was rubbing her head. "Headache?"

"Throw some volts through *your* brain and see what happens."

He stroked her damp hair away from her face. "I have an idea."

"What?"

"Do you trust me, kitten?"

She looked up with a frown as he constructed the fantasy in his mind, projecting it into hers before she could form a protest.

"Oh, hell yeah." Ruby moaned. Those talented, strong fingers she loved worked their oily way up from her calves to the backs of her thighs. "*That's* what I'm talking about."

"Glad you like it."

She opened one sleepy eye to see Leo grinning down at her, his shoulders moving as he expertly massaged her legs. "What are you *really* doing to me?"

Leo shrugged but kept going. "Antibiotic cream. Luckily none of the scrapes are bad. You won't scar."

She snorted. "Glad I can't feel *that*."

"I should never have left you alone."

The condemnation in his voice made her sigh. "I'm alive. You're alive. Kaitlynn is...?"

She looked over her shoulder to see a grim, satisfied smile on Leo's lips. "Dead."

"Good. Did it hurt?"

"A lot."

She laid her head back down on the pillow with a relieved sigh. "Good." She relaxed into his hands, moaning when they moved up to the backs of her thighs. "By the way, could you, um, *not* do the squish thing again?"

"The squish...oh."

"Yeah." She shuddered, swallowing against a fresh wave of nausea.

"I was angry."

She picked her head back up off the pillow and stared at him. "Remind me not to get you mad at me."

His face turned red. He moved up to massage the cheeks of her ass. "I've never tapped into my leprechaun half before. I didn't realize I would do that, let alone could do that."

She nodded and put her head back down, closing her eyes, enjoying the feel of his wonderful hands gliding in soothing strokes over her waist. "I think lessons from Daddy are in order, don't you?"

"Not a bad idea, especially since we'll be so close."

His absent tone said he wasn't really paying attention. She was, however. "Oh? How close are we going to be, Leo?"

His hands stopped. "Um. Yes. About that."

Ruby groaned. "Keep massaging, pretty boy. It sounds like you've got some explaining to do."

"I claimed the land."

His hands found a particularly sore spot. "Oh. That's nice."

"It is?"

"What happened, Leo?"

"I claimed the land, obfuscated everyone's senses but yours, Jaden's and Duncan's, got into the house, and saved the day."

"Oh. Is that all?"

He choked on a laugh. "Yeah. That's all."

"Your brother and sister are safe?"

"Yes, they're fine."

He began massaging her shoulders. She sank into the mattress, her muscles releasing even more tension under his expert hands. "Ohhhh...good."

"If you weren't injured I'd make you feel very, *very* good."

She smiled. "I believe you would."

He pressed a soft kiss to the back of her neck and settled down next to her. "Once those scrapes heal, I'll show you exactly how good I can make you feel."

She stared into his face, the loving expression he wore not fooling her for a moment. "You're going to make me live in Nebraska, aren't you?"

He winced.

"Don't think I didn't catch that whole 'I claimed the land' stuff you said before. You're good, but you're not *that* good."

His eyes narrowed. "Was that a challenge?"

She grinned and pressed a soft kiss to his lips. "Double-dog dare you."

He leaned over her and took her mouth with savage possession. "You're on."

"Oh, boy."

He laughed and the world swirled in mist around her.

Red satin sheets, a black metal headboard, chains and leather cuffs met her gaze. "Uh, Leo?" She pulled on one cuffed wrist, grateful he was blocking the pain of her scrapes. "How is this supposed to work?"

She was on her stomach, a pillow under her hips, canting them upwards. Her legs were also tied, but there was more length to the chain, enabling her to move them a bit more freely.

She couldn't see him, only hear him as he prowled around at the foot of the bed. "Oh, from where I am, it works perfectly." The bed dipped beneath her. He crawled up her body, barely touching her. She felt him caress her ass, cupping it in both hands. "What a beautiful ass."

She would have laughed at his satisfied sigh, but he chose that moment to begin circling her clit. "Oh, God."

"Mmm. You're already getting wet for me." She felt his warm, wet tongue lap between her pussy lips. "So sweet."

Her knees jerked, trying to pull herself up so that she knelt, but the bonds prevented it. "Leo."

He didn't answer. He continued to nibble and suck between her legs while his fingers kept a steady rhythm on her clit. When he leaned back she moaned in denial, her hands straining against her bonds.

"Shh. It's okay, kitten." She heard a buzzing noise, and shivered. "I know what to do to make you purr."

The vibrator worked its way into her pussy. She felt something brush her clit, rabbit ears she thought he'd called them. The vibrator slipped out, taking the rabbit ears off her aching clit. "Do that again."

His dark chuckle was followed by another thrust of the

vibrator. "Do you like that?"

"Yes." She thrust back, trying to get that one piece of the vibrator against her clit again, loving the fullness of the fake cock.

His tongue swiped across her hip. "Want more?" He withdrew the vibrator again.

"Yes!" She was practically hissing at him. He was teasing her with that damn vibrator. She'd have to think of a suitable way to get back at him. Later. Much later.

"I don't know." Once again he pushed the vibrator into her. He twisted it, causing the attachment to brush back and forth, back and forth against her throbbing clit. "This is merely *good*." He leaned over her body until they were eye to eye, his chest to her back, his head resting next to hers on the pillow. His rock hard cock was nestled in the crack of her ass. "Wasn't the dare to make it *very* good?"

She shuddered, an orgasm rippling through her. She was really beginning to like those rabbit ears. He kissed her, his tongue fucking into her mouth. His hips began moving, stroking that hard, hot flesh against her ass.

He twisted the vibrator again, and she nearly jumped off the bed. "Fuck."

"I guess you do like that." He nipped at her neck, sucking hard. She knew he'd left a mark by the way he stared at her, his expression hot and possessive. "Do you know what I'm going to do to you now?"

She felt the head of his cock brush against the entrance to her ass, but she didn't care. The vibrator was beginning to work its magic again. Her fingers curled around the chains tying her to the bed. "Fuck me, Leo."

He shivered. "My pleasure."

If she hadn't been on the verge of orgasm, the feral heat in his tone would have scared the shit out of her.

She felt something cool and wet against her ass, and knew where he was going to fuck her. The lube eased the way for his fingers thrusting in and out, stretching her. The feeling got tighter, wider, the pleasure darkly delicious. His fingers were scissoring her open in preparation for his cock. Between his fingers and the vibrator, she felt stuffed full.

She turned her head when his fingers left her ass. She watched as he greased his cock, his hot gaze glued to her ass. His other hand continued to stroke the vibrator in and out, the occasional twist of his wrist making her shake and moan.

"I'm going to fuck your ass now." He leaned over her again as his thick erection slid between her ass cheeks, the head invading her. He gave the dildo a last violent spin, sending her screaming into orgasm again. His cock sank deep into her ass and she pushed out against him, easing his way. She barely felt the sting, the pleasure drowning out the faint pain of his invasion.

He was peppering her neck and back with tiny kisses. "So tight."

"Leo." She was gasping, the fullness of his cock and the vibrator almost too much to bear.

His teeth sank into her shoulder, just where it joined her neck, his mouth sucking forcefully. He pulled his cock almost all the way out of her. Her back arched, her neck tilting to the side, trying desperately to get him closer. His tongue stroked over the mark he'd left.

He began to move, fucking her with smooth, steady strokes, the vibrator once again brushing against her clit. She found herself rocking back into him, moaning in time to his thrusts.

"So good. So damn good." His words were slurred as he

Dare to Believe

picked up speed, his cock slamming into her. He sat up, both hands on her hips, pummeling her, pulling her ass back to meet him. The vibrator began moving again, somehow obeying his mental commands, driving in and out in counterpoint to his thrusts. The vibrations were driving her insane.

Leo began fucking her hard, the wet slap of flesh against flesh loud in the room. The vibrator was pressed up firmly against her clit, increasing in intensity. Golden sparkles dazzled her eyes, Leo's magic slipping from his grasp to color the air around them.

She could barely breathe as the orgasm washed over her. It burst inside her, devouring her, all of her muscles clenching against the dark pleasure of two cocks. It was almost more than her body could take.

"Ruby! Ah, God!" Leo ground against her ass with a harsh groan and came, the wet warmth sliding into her ass. They shook together, his power blinding them with pleasure so intense Ruby damn near passed out.

He caught himself on his hands as the last of her spasms washed over her. He pulled out, careful not to hurt her. The room drifted away in white mist.

She was back in the Malmayne house. Her ass hurt, her back hurt, her legs and arms hurt, but damn if she didn't care. "I need to double-dog dare you more often." She was still panting, a silly grin on her face.

"Did I hurt you?"

She snuggled down into the pillow, content, and answered him the best way she knew how. She wasn't surprised when he started laughing. After all, he *did* promise to make her purr.

187

"Have you found your father?" Leo stared out the window of the library, hoping Duncan wasn't going to ask him to pinpoint the gravesite. He would, if necessary, but he'd had enough of death for one day.

"He's been found."

Leo turned to see Duncan staring into a whiskey glass. The new Lord of the Malmayne clan swirled the amber liquid around in his glass, his gaze sad and thoughtful. "If I had been here none of this would have happened."

"No offence, but why weren't you?"

Duncan put the drink down carefully on one of the cherry wood tables. His fingers played with the edges of the glass. "My father was still my lord. He sent me to France to deal with some issues we were having with one of our businesses there. It turns out it was nothing more than some members of the clan taking more tithe than they were due. I straightened it out and came back as soon as possible."

"Why didn't any of my calls get through?"

Duncan turned to Jaden. The vampire was currently sprawled on the sofa, his long legs splayed wide, his hands behind his head as he contemplated the ceiling. "I'm not sure, but my cell didn't work the entire time I was in France. As soon as I left for England it suddenly started working again."

"Gremlins?"

"I'm not sure. There are other reasons it might not have worked. I wasn't all that close to Paris, after all. It might have simply been poor signal strength."

"And it might have been the Deranged Darling's hirelings."

The two men shared a look Leo couldn't quite interpret. It was as if they were communicating silently. "It's possible you're right." Duncan picked up his whiskey glass and saluted Leo.

Dare to Believe

"I'm glad we were able to help you rescue your lady."

"Although he didn't need all that much help." Jaden shuddered. "How long is it going to take you to get West out of your ceiling, anyway?"

Leo grimaced. "Please don't mention that again."

"You could just leave him there. Have the column tricked out in concrete. Paint pictures on it. Raise a toast every year in my name. You know, ding, dong, the asshole's dead."

Leo shook his head at the happily humming vampire. He turned to Duncan, who was smiling down at his bond brother. "Is he always like that?"

"Frequently." Duncan took a drink of his whiskey. "What are your plans now?"

"Now? Learn how to control my leprechaun side, apparently." He glanced up and saw Ruby step cautiously into the library, her gaze going warily back and forth between Duncan and Jaden. She was dressed in one of his shirts. Luckily it was long enough on her to hit just above her knees. He moved forward, eager to take his mate into his arms. "And plan a wedding."

Even as she nestled into his arms, she was arguing. "You're planning the wedding? Try we're planning the wedding. And no getting freaky in front of my relatives." She looked around Leo's shoulder to glare at Jaden. "I'm talking to you especially, fang boy."

"Fang boy? First you call me Bunnicula, and now fang boy?"

Bunnicula? Leo laughed. "You invited the Hob to the wedding, and you're worried about a vampire?"

He could hear Duncan choking on his whiskey even as Jaden sputtered. "The Hob? She invited *the Hob* to your wedding? With *humans*?" The vampire doubled over in laughter, gasping. "Oh, man, I am *so* there."

And all Leo could do was agree and kiss his wife.

He was *so* there.

Epilogue

Jaden watched as Leo, Ruby and the Dunne family were reunited. *Ah, family bonding down on the farm.* He snorted, amused. He wondered what they were going to say when he told them Moira was coming with him, whether they liked it or not. He had the feeling they wouldn't take that very well.

Too bad, so sad. He'd decided to claim Moira as his own, and no one was going to stand in his way. He climbed out of the limo into the night, thankful that Dunne had been willing to wait until Jaden could accompany them. While sunlight wouldn't kill him outright, it would make him damn sick. Accommodating his "allergy" wasn't something most Fae, Sidhe or not, would bother with, but Dunne had made an exception.

Guess he feels he owes me. Yeah, well, Jaden planned on taking payment in the form of the man's sister.

"May I exit the limo, Jaden?"

Jaden smiled. "Sorry, Duncan." He stepped aside, his eyes never leaving Moira. The evening did wonders for her. She glowed under the light of the newly risen moon. She was casting looks his way, too, her eyes flickering back and forth between him and Duncan, a wariness present he'd do his best to remove before too much time had passed. He sent reassurances, and love, down the link, and watched her relax.

He stepped forward, hoping against hope that she wouldn't reject him. She represented everything he'd ever wanted in a female. She was strong, spirited, beautiful, and loyal. He couldn't wait to make her his. The light bond he'd established with her had let him feel everything she did, all that she was, and as far as he was concerned she was glorious.

Duncan stepped in front of Moira, a stunned expression on his face. Jaden's heart nearly stopped. Down the bond he felt a shock of recognition.

No.

Duncan bent down and tasted Moira's sweet lips.

Fuck. This can't be happening!

But it was.

His bond-brother had found his mate.

Now what the hell was Jaden supposed to do? He'd bonded with Duncan's *mate!* And the Sidhe were not known for sharing, especially with a vampire, no matter how chummy they'd gotten over the years. Jaden collapsed against the limo with a smothered groan.

Well. Fuck a duck.

Duncan had Moira up in his arms and in the limo before she could even form a protest. Jaden watched, torn between amusement, envy and jealousy. His Lordship wasn't even going to give her a chance to say no. Nope, he just packed her in the car and got ready to drive off with her.

Which, admittedly, was what Jaden had planned to do too. Wasn't it nice to know his plan would have worked?

"What the hell do you think you're doing?" Leo's voice was partly stunned, partly amused.

Duncan beamed back at Dunne, his expression lighter than Jaden could ever remember seeing it. Damn it. "Claiming my mate." He climbed into the limo and gestured for Jaden to join him.

Jaden shook his head, making sure the amusement was all Duncan would see. He couldn't afford for Duncan to feel *exactly* what Jaden was going through. "Nah." He took a deep breath. He could do this. "There's some unfinished business here that needs tending to. I'll meet up with you later. Besides, you two need some alone time." He gave Duncan his best leer and tried to mask his true emotions.

No way in hell could he watch the two of them together. He was happy for them both, but damn. He wasn't really into masochism. And seeing what he couldn't be a part of would kill something inside him.

Some of Duncan's happiness dimmed. "But, Jaden—"

He shut the door to the limo without even looking, cutting Duncan off mid-protest, and strode towards the Dunne's. He ignored Duncan's call in his mind, pushing him away as gently as he could. Moira's link was weak enough that he shut her out without too much effort. They needed to be alone, and he needed to keep his nose, and his freaky vampire brain, out of it. *Three's a crowd, right?*

Blech. I hate being noble. He so desperately wanted to climb into that limo, rip both their clothes off and have some fun, but he couldn't. Not only had Duncan never indicated any interest in the male of the species, he'd just begun to claim his *mate*. And Jaden loved them both enough to want them happy.

Still, this sucks big moose dick.

He patted the hood of the limo and nodded to the driver before turning and walking away. "Evening, folks. I understand you have some questions." He grinned as wickedly as he knew how, throwing every ounce of cockiness he had left into it. "Lucky me. I have answers."

He tried to ignore the crack in his heart as the limo pulled away, taking with it the only people he'd ever loved.

About the Author

Dana Marie Bell wrote her first short story when she was thirteen years old. She attended the High School for Creative and Performing Arts for creative writing, where freedom of expression was the order of the day. When her parents moved out of the city and placed her in a Catholic high school for her senior year she tried desperately to get away, but the nuns held fast, and she graduated with honors despite herself.

Dana has lived primarily in the Northeast (Pennsylvania, New Jersey and Delaware, to be precise), with a brief stint on the US Virgin Island of St. Croix. She lives with her soul-mate and husband Dusty, their two maniacal children, an evil ice-cream stealing cat and a bull terrier that thinks it's a Pekinese.

You can learn more about Dana at: www.danamariebell.com

Brotherly love? Oh hell *no…*

Kiss and Kin
© 2009 Kinsey W. Holley

On the surface, court reporter Lark Manning looks like the luckiest girl in the world, blessed with great friends and a wonderful family. Underneath, she harbors a hopelessly unrequited love for the sexy werewolf everyone thinks of as her cousin. Taran rarely notices her except to condescend or lecture. He's treated her the same way since she was eight years old, and there's no reason to think he'll ever change.

Taran Lloyd, a detective in the Houston Police Department's Shifters Investigations Unit (SIU), lives for those rare moments he gets to spend around Lark, torturing himself with what he can't have. Kin only by marriage, she thinks of him as her big brother. He couldn't bear her pity—or her disgust—if she learned he wants her for his mate.

When weres from a rival pack attack her, Lark screams out the first name that comes to mind—Taran. Only this sexy alpha can keep her safe until they find out who wants her dead, and why. But keeping her safe means keeping her close. And the closer they get, the harder it gets for these not-really-cousins to honor their commitment to keep their paws off.

Warning: Contains a heroine with the world's worst poker face, a hero with more honor than sense, and explicit shifter sex that makes you wish werewolves really were part of the gene pool.

Available now in ebook from Samhain Publishing.
Also available in the print anthology Shifting Dreams from Samhain Publishing.

Think it's glamorous being a vampire? Think again.

Called by Blood
© *2009 Evie Byrne*
The Faustin Bros., Book 1

Alexander Faustin is ready to settle down. He travels from NYC to sunny Colorado to find his destined bride. His delicate mission: to explain to her that vamps exist, that he happens to be one himself, and that he'd like her to be one, too. But the moment he lays eyes on Helena MacAllister, talk is the last thing on his mind.

It's not like Helena to make out with a stranger on her front porch, much less invite him into her bed. Somehow Alex makes her feel safe, even while he's dismantling her defenses. But in the wake of an accident, her faith in him is shattered. She learns her dream lover is a monster.

When a vampire betrays and terrifies his beloved, what can he offer her to make it up? Pancakes, of course. It's a start, at least. And Alex has to think of the next step quick, because if Helena won't take him back, he'll never love again.

Warning: Contains graphic sex scenes, blood play, and one scene of voyeurism. There's also a scary part in the middle. The author and her lawyers remind you that this is a work of fiction. In real life, a one-night stand with a stalker is a bad idea, unless the stalker is a vampire, in which case it's an amazingly bad idea. (Note: No actual elk were harmed in the writing of this novella.)

Available now in ebook from Samhain Publishing.

Is Emma ready for a bite?

The Wallflower
© *2008 Dana Marie Bell*
A Hunting Love story
Halle Puma Series Book 1

Emma Carter has been in love with Max Cannon since high school, but he barely knew she existed. Now she runs her own unique curio shop, and she's finally come out her shell and into her own.

When Max returns to his small home town to take up his duties as the Halle Pride's Alpha, he finds that shy little Emma has grown up. That small spark of something he'd always felt around the teenager has blossomed into something more—his mate!

Taking her "out for a bite" ensures that the luscious Emma will be permanently his.

But Max's ex has plans of her own. Plans that don't include Emma being around to interfere. To keep her Alpha, Emma must prove to the Pride that she has what it takes to be Max's mate.

Warning: This title contains explicit sex, graphic language, loads of giggles and a hot, blond Alpha male.

Available now in ebook from Samhain Publishing.
Also available in the print anthology Hunting Love from Samhain Publishing.

My Bookstore & More

www.mybookstoreandmore.com

Green for the planet.
Great for your wallet.

GREAT CHEAP FUN

Discover eBooks!

THE FASTEST WAY TO GET THE HOTTEST NAMES

Get your favorite authors on your favorite reader, long before they're out in print! Ebooks from Samhain go wherever you go, and work with whatever you carry—Palm, PDF, Mobi, and more.

Samhain Publishing ltd

WWW.SAMHAINPUBLISHING.COM

Breinigsville, PA USA
16 November 2010
249450BV00004B/1/P